TINY
NIGHT
MARES

ALSO BY LINCOLN MICHEL AND
NADXIELI NIETO

*Tiny Crimes: Very Short Tales of
Mystery & Murder*

Gigantic Worlds

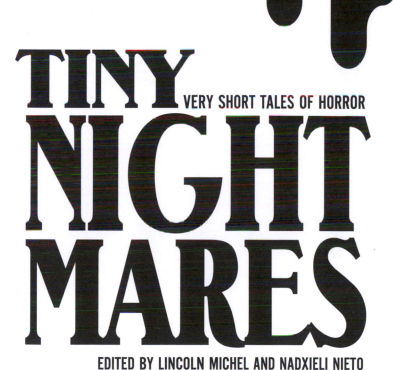

TINY

VERY SHORT TALES OF HORROR

NIGHT MARES

EDITED BY LINCOLN MICHEL AND NADXIELI NIETO

NEW YORK
CATAPULT

Anthology selection copyright © 2020 by Lincoln Michel and Nadxieli Nieto

ISBN: 978-1-948226-62-2

Interior illustrations by Daehyun Kim
Cover and book design by Nadxieli Nieto

Library of Congress Control Number: 2020931219

Printed in Hong Kong
10 9 8 7 6 5 4 3 2 1

For all of us, screaming in horror

CONTENTS

LIMBS

VISCERA

ILLUSTRATIONS • **DAEHYUN KIM**

INTRODUCTION

An argument can be made that fear made humans what we are. Literally. Our eyes evolved to see monsters lurking in the grass, our ears to hear creatures going bump in the night. Fear is also, for better or (more often) worse, the dark force that shapes society. Whether it's politicians spreading hatred to scare up votes or the passive fear that keeps so many of us from risking change in our lives, our communities, and our world.

In *Tiny Nightmares* we've asked some of our favorite authors what scares them. These stories—from forty-two of the most exciting writers of horror and literary fiction—wander through a vast forest of horror: from ride-sharing murders and mind-reading witches to fears of childbirth and funhouse marriages from which there is no escape. They wrest from the shadows not only vampires and werewolves but also the terrors of the waking world—racism, sexism, online radicalization, economic instability, environmental disaster.

In the shadow of these larger systemic horrors, tiny nightmares breed. These nightmares, masked and unmasked, provoke a deeper dread and implicate the reader. We are often the very thing another rightfully fears.

For creatures shaped by fear, horror stories hold a unique place. They can explore the dark cracks and dank corners of life, making us see more clearly. Many of our oldest stories are, in a sense, horror stories. Fairy tales and myths are full of terrifying transformations, hidden evils, and dire warnings about what lurks in the dark woods just outside of town. Despite this, horror fiction is still too often dismissed.

For *Tiny Nightmares*, we wanted to poke another hole in the artificial barrier between "literary" and "genre" fiction. We've collected more than forty stories from established authors of both worlds as well as emerging writers who we're confident you'll be seeing more of in the years to come. We have divided the book loosely into four parts, four body parts naturally—Heads, Hearts, Limbs, and Viscera—loosely held together by sinews of weirdness. The stories here are small in size—each under 1,500 words—but the nightmares are large. Each story is a tiny crack in the door to which we press our eye, unsure of what we will find staring back at us.

We hope you enjoy.

Sincerely,
Lincoln Michel and Nadxieli Nieto

Guess

MEG ELISON

Nobody likes it when we're right. Not the guess-your-age guy, not the guess-your-weight guy, and certainly not me. The age guy, well, he's never right. Because people are more likely to play along if he guesses they're ten years younger than they are. He loses bullshit eight-cent prizes made in China and he keeps taking a dollar from every idiot in his line. The weight guy is right more often. He gets away with it because the skinny people are proud of themselves and the fat people are a source of entertainment, no matter what he says. He's right, he's wrong, they're still fat.

Then they come around to me. And I am never wrong.

Sometimes I think I can do some good. Whenever I say "lung cancer," the person I'm talking to says they'll quit. If I say "liver failure," it goes the same way. That one guy I told it would be a plane crash said he'd never fly again, but I don't know if he stuck by it. I also don't know if a plane crashed into his house while he was asleep. But what about the ones I tell it'll be a car accident? What the hell are they supposed to do?

When Dad did it, he told people to try to take comfort in heart failure, in knowing how the end will come. "It's the one thing in life you can count on," he'd say. "And now you'll know its name when it shows up. Isn't that the definition of comfort? Familiarity?"

Dad didn't do it at the carnival. Dad had a real job. He'd do it for friends and family, he'd do it a year before it happened, or twenty. He was right about everybody, including himself (pancreatic cancer). After he was gone, I saw that he was right about his sister, his best friend, our dog. That's how I know I am never wrong.

I don't know how we count as fun, us guessers. It isn't a game. There's no clown to shoot with a water pistol and there's no ring to toss. The prizes are shitty and the truth is nobody's friend. And tonight smells like candy corn and puke, and this town is like every other.

Patty, 48, 287 pounds, will die of complications from an amputated foot. She leaves with her face in a twist and goes straight to the cotton candy man. I never know when, but I suspect for her that it will be soon.

Bill, 36, 215 pounds, will die in an industrial accident involving molten metal. His face when I say that to him. Jesus.

Alex, 23, 117 pounds, will die of an autoimmune disorder. Does not seem surprised.

Gus, 14, 98 pounds, will drown. God, I hate it when kids walk in here.

On and on, every night, their dazed faces all blurring into one.

Except.

Except the carnival is heading south as the summer ends. We're chasing the heat and barreling toward our stopping point in Galveston. I'm working a cruise ship when we get there.

The age guy changed his accent to sound Southern as soon as we hit the Mason-Dixon Line. The weight guy is gearing up for Southern women who don't ever wanna play at all, and most certainly don't want to hear the truth when they're made to.

And I can't do accents and I can't lie, so the last few weeks on the road have been real weird for me. Ever since Tulsa, I'm stuck.

Shirley, 56, 186 pounds, will die of thirst.

Caiden, 21, 125 pounds, will die of thirst.

Evan, 28, 146 pounds, will die of thirst.

My line dries up right away. They think I'm being an asshole. I can feel sweat collecting in the small of my back and rolling down. The night is way too warm. My mouth feels sticky like cotton candy.

Oklahoma City and it's midnight and still above ninety degrees.

Lorna, 39, 159 pounds, thirst.

Jake, 47, 180 pounds, thirst.

Bobby, 5, 41 pounds, thirst.

This crowd is drunker and thinks I'm joking. They drink more, they suggest I drink more. I am beginning to think we should drink all there is while we still can.

Galveston is where I figure it out. I haven't kept up with the news while we've been on the road, and when I get it, it's almost too hysterical to figure out. All the papers are saying the same thing. The bill is coming due. We've been putting off doing something about this for years and now it's too late.

I look up at the seagulls at the marina and I know what they'll all die of. Thirst.

I never make it to the cruise ship. Some asshole sees me doing my act at our last stop and he finds me. Tells me he's too smart to die of thirst, and he's right. He says he knows what I am. He says I need to come with him and he says a number that makes up my mind for me.

I've been on this ship now for six months and I don't think I'll ever get off it. They have some of the best dew-collecting and condensing machines in the world. The ship is comfortable. The food is fresh; there are hydroponics on board and they know what they're doing. But I never see them. The man who brought me here keeps me locked up in my room and visits me once a day. He won't let anyone else in here. He says I'm his surety against the inevitable end.

Knowing might be a comfort, but it isn't a surety. And

there still might be time to change this. But I know what I know, and I and everyone on this ship will die of a gunshot wound. Soon.

The man who brought me here is named Chris. He's about forty-five and I'd say a buck thirty soaking wet. And he's going to die after drinking a poison that is neither as painless nor as quick as he was told it would be.

I am never wrong.

Rearview

SAMANTHA HUNT

Starlings loop overhead. It's a cloud of birds. Part of the flock disappears as light on light. The other part blackens the pale sky like a finger reversing velvet.

A mother and daughter, humans, watch the birds' rigid coordination. The flock makes a low rumbling sound as if the birds, taken together, are one thing rather than many. A hive. A body. A mind. If the humans knew the word for this flock, a murmuration of starlings, they'd understand now how these birds got the name. But these humans know very little. Their mobile devices are not working. There's no connection.

"They never collide?" the daughter asks.

Her mother shrugs.

Birds twist. It's dangerous, wonderful. It's fearfully unanimous, or just plain fearful, when many think and act like one.

"Maybe a falcon's near and they're scared shitless." The mother doesn't usually swear in front of her daughter. "Poopless, I mean." The birds are directly over their heads. Poopless could be a good thing.

Earlier: Mother and daughter drive through the night. The mother breathes audibly to calm herself, but she's not calm. The mother checks to see what might be following them. She catches sight of her daughter asleep in the backseat. All that's precious; life, sleep, breathing. The rear window is a square of darkness, a black screen. There's much the mother doesn't remember, dark squares in her own brain. Anything at all might be following them.

At a rest stop the mother destroys her mobile phone in the toilet.

Back on the road she tunes the radio. Announcers banter. They say so many dumb things, scripts that follow a bad idea of what it means to be a man, what it means to be a woman. Giggles. Teasing. Nonsense to fill the airwaves. There's a story about how our past digital lives—old status updates and social media posts—will haunt us forever. Everything stupid we ever did. Everything cruel continues to exist as part of the public record, forever. *"A young man lost his job when the bosses found photos of him urinating on a friend's head. Not a good friend, I hope. Hahaha."*

"Oh, Mike! You're bad! You're so bad!"

It hasn't rained in a long time.

The mother exits the highway. Her e-toll pays the debt.

The town is a remote mountain holiday spot in the off-season. The shops are closed except for a grocery. The mother pulls over for human supplies. They will need food. They will need water.

The tires stop spinning, stop lulling. The daughter wakes. Alone in the car, she reaches for her phone without thought. It's what she does. She texts a boyfriend. It's late. He forgets himself. He writes, *Send me dirty pix.* The girl considers his request. A shadowy breast shot might be nice. Mother returns. Daughter hides her phone.

"Where are we, Mom?"

They arrive at a cabin deep in the woods. It's surrounded by infinite pines, maples, oaks, trees of all sorts. There are no other houses. No power lines. Just the woods. Underneath the trees, deep in the soil, fungi attach themselves to the trees' roots. These mushrooms, though really it is one big mushroom, suck some of the tree's sugar from the roots. In return they serve as a telephone operator for the forest. They connect one tree's roots to its neighbor's to its neighbor's. Trees communicate through the fungus. They do not speak English. They do not speak in words humans would understand.

The door to the cabin is padlocked, so the mother smashes the lock with the lip of a shovel left on the landing.

"Mom!" The daughter's surprised her mom had it in her. Like a professional bad guy. Breaking and entering.

The lock gives easily. Mother and daughter inch into the dark cabin.

"Where are we, Mom?" Again.

"Shhhh."

They sleep wrapped like spoons in a room where mounted deer watch the bed, watch them sleep.

The sun rises. The daughter takes a short walk to a dock on a quiet lake. No one's there. She snaps some photos of the lake and attempts to post them but there's no coverage. There's no connection. The starlings soar overhead. Her mother joins her at the dock. They drink coffee. The birds obey silent commands. The birds make their murmur without even trying. It's a chorus, a group, a pixelated mob blurring to one.

Near sunset, mother and daughter prepare a small meal. They build a fire in the cabin. They burn wood. They warm a can of beans and nibble on some cheese.

"Before GPS," the mother says, "lost was possible. You could not know where you were. No one could find you. Before. You have no idea."

The daughter nods. "Where are we?"

Mother ignores. "Also," she says, "clocks could be wrong. Like, the clock in your car might be ten minutes fast or a watch could run slow. Things could be inaccurate. Different. Not like now."

The daughter's cell phone rings.

"I said no electronics."

"It's just Tony, Mom." The boyfriend.

The mother grabs the ringing phone. There are no bars, no connection. The mother's hand trembles. She answers. "Hello?" No one's there. Or no one who speaks is there.

The mother throws the phone into the fire.

In the night the mother wakes. Someone is in their room. The past does not have to try hard to find us, especially not at night. So the mother isn't surprised. "You found us," she whispers. "The phone?"

"I'll always find you," the person says.

The mother pulls the bedcovers up over her body, making a poor shield.

"I am you." The stranger approaches the bed. Her face is revealed in the low light. The stranger is not a stranger. She is the mother, only younger and skinny as a junkie.

"Please," the mother says. "I'm clean now. I'm a mother now."

Junkie shrugs. She sits on the edge of the bed, prepping a syringe. "You tried to kill me," she says. She pulls down the bedcovers, like a lover accessing the mother's body, her body.

"Don't. Please." It's a whisper. But the mother lies still. Maybe she is crying. Maybe she is grateful. She hasn't had a hit of anything in years.

The mother does not fight. The drug enters her blood. She convulses, a worm. She nods off, asleep or asleep-like.

Her arm is pierced by the syringe and a history that never leaves, a history so haunted. The arm lands across her daughter's sleeping body with a hard thud.

The daughter wakes to two mothers. "Who are you? What are you doing?" she asks the younger one.

The junkie smiles.

"Mom?" The daughter shakes the mother in bed beside her, trying to wake the mother she knows. "What did you do?" The daughter lunges at the intruder. She attacks, but the junkie mother is cruel and desperate. She fights viciously. And the daughter can't bring herself to fight very hard at all. What if she hurts her mother? What if she hurts her mother before her mother has a chance to become her mother?

The junkie has no such restraint. With full fists the junkie swings, beating her daughter horribly, saying awful things to her own child, things like, "We never wanted you." She hits and kicks and spits. The daughter, bloody and bruised, tucks into a protective curl on the floor. The junkie laughs above, landing another boot in the daughter's side. She pulls back again, ready to strike.

But then, an unsettling crack, a vessel split open like the padlock, like a memory. The junkie crumples to the ground.

The daughter uncurls in the silence and looks up to see her protector, a young girl, only seven years old. The shovel is raised in the little girl's hand. The daughter squints at the girl. "Mom?" she asks her.

"Yeah, honey," the little girl says. "Yeah. It's me. Everything's going to be all right."

"It is?" the daughter asks.

But the young girl says nothing. She's caught, or confused by a program or stuck a moment, two moments. Processing. Processing. There is no connection.

Grimalkin

ANDREW F. SULLIVAN

The kitten climbs up and out of my sister's mouth in the middle of the night, emerging as one long strand of hair and bone. I watch as it draws a wet tail past her lips and then drops to the floor, stretching out on the ragged red carpet between our twin beds.

Most nights, I'm asleep before this happens. I don't hear the kitten scratching at the bedposts. I don't notice her leaping up onto the sill, tracking the moon with pale yellow eyes. Tonight, I watch her body flatten out, slipping through the cracked window we leave open for her no matter the season. I listen to her, waiting for a voice to whisper back at me, *go to sleep*. She is hunting, searching for sustenance before the sun comes out again. I don't speak a word. I know the rules.

Grandma hates to be interrupted.

•

The promise was to keep her safe. After they found her circle in the basement, Grandma knew her days were numbered in this town. Our mother claimed ignorance and disbelief, joined the chorus of voices calling for her head. Our father sealed himself away in his room, the television drowning out any thought of his mother, her life threatened by familiar faces and strangers alike whenever she left the house. Her car was set on fire. It burned for hours. No one put it out. We were told not to visit, not to speak, not to smile. We were told to be afraid.

She came to us in the middle of the night, her form new and unpolished. The tail ended in a ball of gluey fur, the ears were shaped like raw bat wings, pink and pulsing with tiny veins.

You can save me, she said. You can protect me.

My sister and I stared, each tucked into bed, quivering beneath the covers.

Only you can do this, she said. The voice was bigger than her shape.

Do this, she said in the growing darkness. Do this, and I will show you everything.

Grandma had no daughter of her own. She told us she was not blessed. Grandpa cared only about amassing things—money, property, power. All three one and the same eventually, Grandma said. She was cursed to have one son and only one son. A boy spoiled by his father, a boy unable to understand his place in the world, as everywhere he went he was placed upon a pedestal. A shiftless and ungrateful boy who let his father's empire of car dealerships and repair shops fall into dust while barely flinching in the process. This explained our shared room, our twin beds, our rotten red carpet that felt wet even when it was dry in the morning.

Our birth offered her a new chance to pass on what her mother had taught her, old ways of power, old ways of knowing the world. Sometimes they required blood and sometimes they required flame, but they were true and honest. They did not take without reason. They demanded sacrifice, but demands were proportionate. The balance was retained. The balance was essential.

We offer a balance, my sister and I. Two strands of the same soul, spun into mirrored shapes, spun into soft and malleable flesh. We could push these powers further. We could become more.

I waited my whole life for you two, Grandma said. And now they want to take me from you.

When she returns, I stare at the ceiling. After she has fed on mice or birds or smaller things, her tiny body bloats like a tumor. Her hunger is constant and inevitable. Without her nightly feed, she cannot live like this, tucked deep inside our chests, keeping time against our hearts. We take turns, alternating month to month as the moon shifts and the tides change. My turn is coming again. I will dream behind her eyes as she stalks the night, listening for her prey, hunting the weak, the stupid, and the maimed. I will dream in red and pink and white, white bone.

Before climbing back onto my sister's chest, she leaves small bones from her kill for us on the carpet. We will grind those bones up into a powder, a powder the keeper will swirl into a glass of water before bed, the spell requiring our participation, our ingestion of the dead. We tell our mother it is for our bowel movements, and she approves. She wants us to be regular.

I stare at the ceiling and listen to the sound of Grandma sliding back down my sister's throat.

Tomorrow, a new cycle begins. I can already taste the dead in my mouth, the particles clinging to the back of my throat like sand. Tomorrow, I must become the keeper once again.

The spells are small and easy. They are more like charms and incantations. A burst of energy in the mornings after we set the charred sticks in the correct configuration, burn the right herbs in the backyard, telling our father it's for chemistry class. Our memories improve together, our recall for formulas and history transforming our test scores. Sometimes we answer wrong on purpose, to protect us from suspicion. Grandma says like any gambler, we must know when to walk away, when to make a mistake that everyone can see. We must sow doubt if we want to reap her rewards. We must seem human. We must be plausible.

I watch my sister growing tired as the months pass, see

her fading every time her month arrives, the burden in her chest drying out her skin, puckering the corners of her eyes. Grandma says it's the stress of keeping a secret, the wear and tear of the lie working itself across our bodies. She says what we're doing is beautiful and necessary, sacred even. When I find my sister puking in the grass behind our school, Grandma says we should be grateful she has chosen us.

Tonight I take the powder, swirl it around the glass. I stand before the mirror and then watch myself raise the glass to my lips, watch myself pause and then pour it all down the drain.

My sister is already asleep in the other room, worn out by her month incubating Grandma. The role of the keeper is not easy. It takes and takes and takes. The deal we have made is not proportionate. We can feel the years slipping away, the time passing us by, the time she is taking until she can seize one of us. We talk about this in whispers, wondering if she can hear from within our chests, her long pink ears pressed against our ribs, on alert for any betrayal.

I shut the door and lie down in bed. I leave the window cracked open. I close my eyes and wait for sleep to come. There is no death lingering at the back of my throat, no tiny bits of bone floating in my stomach acid. Grandma will have to fight her way out from inside me tonight, each claw a pin pressed into my lungs. I intend to keep her there until she starves.

Doggy-Dog World

HILARY LEICHTER

I know this couple in a casual way. A neighborly way. They went to the adoption place to adopt a cute friend. Something soft and sweet, something to love. We want something to love, they said, and I said, Besides each other? They said, In addition to. We want something waiting for us by the door. A fan, a witness, this is our wish.

By my front door, I have an antique mirror so I can be my own fan, my own witness.

The first puppy didn't work out. The first puppy was sick and needed people with experience. This couple had a lot of experience, but not the right kind. They cried about the first puppy. I made them an interesting blend of tea and stroked their hair until they felt better.

The second puppy was as tiny as you can imagine. Whatever you're imagining is correct.

Perpetually bouncing, like it could blow away any second, just float up in the air like a cute, flying, cartoon sort of creature. She was a dear little friend, and they loved her very much. They let her sleep in their bed and eat out of their bowls and make messes as long as the messes were on the tile and not the carpet.

One thing: this couple was not super-perceptive. They were not the kind of people who noticed other people. There was the time I cut my hair and they did not see that the hairs were cut. Or the time I was in a car accident and walked on crutches for weeks. After a month, the couple said, Hey, what's with the crutches? There was the time I was in love with this couple, both as a couple and as individuals, loved them in a visible way, an embarrassing way, for years. Then the feelings expired and I felt relaxed, easy. It is sometimes good to go unnoticed.

My point is: when the puppy turned into a human baby, it took them a while to catch on. First the sounds coming from her puppy mouth were baby sounds. Then the paws on her puppy legs were baby paws, which I guess are just called feet. Maybe it was hours before the couple noticed. Maybe it was a whole afternoon. She had maybe already been a baby for a few days before the couple said, *Oh my god*.

Everyone around town was talking. The first thing

I personally do in situations like these is to make myself mindful of precedent. Consider the frog who turns into the prince, and the beast who turns into the prince, and consider all of those princes sprung from the bodies of beasts. Now, consider the puppy who turns into a child, and what sort of suburban spell could have put her in such a difficult spot? I volunteered as babysitter and helped care for her, this very special baby. She was not as bouncy as her former incarnation. She was not a creature who could fly away, in fact, she wouldn't. When describing her, the word that came to mind was *responsible*. I looked into her eyes and found a steadiness I could relate to.

The couple converted their office into a nursery with an air of *Okay, this is what we're doing now!* They replaced the puppy toys with baby toys, the puppy bed with a baby crib. They replaced the dog park with the playground and the poop scoop with a closet full of diapers. They transitioned so naturally from puppy to baby that there was no trace of the puppy I once knew, not at all. The puppy things were in garbage bags in the basement, tucked away in a far corner.

This is the part of the story where the couple started calling themselves *the family*. I should start calling them that too, but I won't, because of what happened to the couple next.

It was at the restaurant across town, the one that serves pieces of toast topped with fancy foods. The couple was on a date, and I was watching their child. The woman from the restaurant who called on the phone said it happened during the third course of the meal, the dessert toasts.

The couple started bickering, but their bickers turned to barks. Their faces went furry and small. They tried to pick up their slabs of bread, but they had dog paws instead of human paws, which I guess are just called hands. The couple was a couple of hounds, noses sniffing plates of expensive carbohydrates.

I strapped the baby to my chest and fetched them from their date. I brought some of the old puppy leashes, and leashed them up, walked them home. I brought the rest of the puppy things up from their basement, and over to my house. I stroked their fur and made them an interesting blend of dried foods to eat, since they had missed their dinner.

I set the two doggie beds near the front door, under my antique mirror. I look at myself when I leave for work, adjust my collar, adjust my skirt. Adjust the stroller and adjust the baby tucked in the stroller. I look at my dogs. I look at my family, all together. I adjust my face, make sure it looks normal, for I, too, have sprung from unexpected things.

Twenty-First-Century Vetala

AMRITA CHAKRABORTY

My last body was a gentle woman, in life. From the small bedsit I lived in then, I used to watch her from across our balconies, humming a Hemanta Mukhopadhyay song as she put the laundry out to dry. Her hands were scarred and always slightly damp, water dripping from them as she cooked or wiped or washed another wanting thing. Because I was, or at least appeared to be, a man she knew as a mere fellow tenant, there was never any true communication between us. Only my curious glances above the books I held out in front of me, looks she was too busy to ever acknowledge, aside from a curt nod if she happened to meet my eyes.

Nor did I pursue that interest any further, at least not until afterward. I'm not like my brother, after all, who found the most striking man in Kolkata and waited it out until he died from a heart attack at forty-two. (Dada's never been clear on whether that was a natural occurrence.) The last time I saw him, he had brought a girl to the graveyard we shared as an occasional local haunt, and she clutched his arm the entire time he spoke with me, giggling uneasily. I doubt he truly enjoys anything about it but their admiration, the thickening sensation of being the center of another's want.

No, I'm not like him. There's little about behaving like a human myself that interests me—I would never wish to be one of them. But I do consider myself somewhat of an expert on the things that drive them to behave the way they do. To feel what they feel. I have worn so many human skins, seen the world through near-infinite pairs of eyes. Sometimes I tire of them and wish I could stuff this stray consciousness, this mass of ephemera, into some species of animal with fewer concerns weighing on it. Or a plant, even a rock. But my kind were made to stay in humanity's shade. To live eternally on the crest of their death.

In the days before Moyna died, I had been just barely clinging to the body of the aging law clerk who rented the flat opposite hers. Despite the delayed decay due to my presence, his skin had started to attain an unnatural green tint, and I could tell that the body was dangerously close to the stage at which the internal organs would burst and begin to leak out, when it would obviously become useless to me. I never stayed past the point when people would notice anything more than a peculiar illness taking hold of their neighborhood loner or the newcomer to town; there are few these days who know the old stories to oust or destroy us but I take no risks when it comes to the survival of our kind. Despite the degradation of my assumed form, though, I found it more difficult than usual to move on. You might guess why.

Moyna was generous with her time and labor, as most women I observe are; giving and giving and scraping the bottom of the well when nothing else is left. Whether this was in her nature or simply her choice to fulfill the needs of those around her—what did that matter? After I first oriented myself in the tenor of her breaths, memorized the particularities of her muscles and neural grooves, I was taken aback by how much was expected of her. That first morning, I couldn't get anything right—not rising by dawn to prepare her husband's humble breakfast of a paratha and mint achar, not getting the children dressed for school, and certainly not the intricacies of preparing food for eight people while doing the washing and caring for an elderly mother-in-law. These difficulties of daily life were precisely why I rarely took hold of bodies like this, indispensable tethers to their families.

Oh, but when it came to Moyna, I could not resist, however inconvenient. How can I explain this to you without resorting to shoddy metaphor? Here: one morning she stood in the doorway to the balcony, her head resting on the chipped wall. She closed her eyes and lifted one hand out of the shadows, as if to cup a measure of sunlight for use in some celestial recipe. Shontu, her three-year-old son, came toddling out to meet his mother, hugging the tail end of her saree. I glanced down at my book then, the moment suddenly too effulgent for my borrowed vision. When I looked up again, she had hoisted the child up onto one hip, and drawn his hand out to meet the sun. Her nose pressed into Shontu's cheek and he laughed, and suddenly, her eyes. Anyone would have wanted to live through them.

I swear I left her behind as kindly as I could. On the pallet that served as her bed, nearing the evening so her husband would find her once he came home from his work at the nearby processing plant. I put her children down for their afternoon nap before I laid her down. The stove stood at attention, a fresh, if awkwardly cooked pot of daal their final gift from her.

Yesterday, my brother met me at the graveyard, and when his new girl drew her arms around him and whispered in his ear, I looked away. I looked into the fiercely sunlit ground.

We've Been in Enough Places to Know

COREY FARRENKOPF

The condos' septic failed. It was among the deficiencies that developed over the first two years of habitation. The paint job peeled around month two. The cellar's cement walls cracked after month six. The HVAC system coughed acrid black smoke on the first cold day in November. The list went on, but the septic was what forced inhabitants out, what prompted the lawsuits over the shoddy construction, forged permits, and the outrageous price residents paid to inhabit the crumbling beachside villa.

The building had begun to lean toward the bay. High tide lapped through backyard decking, dragging the seawall away, speeding erosion. A red X was painted across the front door, situated between two boarded-up windows that Glen knew were Tiffany glass. He'd snapped cell phone shots of the ornate panes from within to show his girlfriend how misplaced the builder's priorities were.

Glen worked for SeaSide Property Management. Twice a week, he walked through each condo looking for squatters. The owner believed he could salvage his business venture before the structure descended into the sea. Glen had his doubts, considering the amount of water in the basement and the veins of mold beneath the peeled paint. Then there was the thing swimming in the basement, drifting between steel Lally columns, the ridge of knotted spine pressing up through the water.

Glen's boss said, *If it's not kids or homeless sleeping in there, best not mention it to the cops.*

Every time Glen walked through the sagging halls, he considered more appropriate land usage. The six-point-two acres could have been left as protected wetland, breeding grounds for waterfowl, a sandy stretch of beach for turtles to lay their eggs. If it had to be housing, why not affordable housing? Fifteen units at several hundred thousand a pop could have been a hundred affordable units for working-class families.

Glen considered renting rooms to kids he went to high school with who griped about the housing shortage online.

No one would know. He was the only employee checking the building. It would be easy to forge requests to have the power turned on. The septic leached only a negligible amount of fecal matter into the surrounding waters.

But Glen couldn't do it. Beyond the environmental sin, the building was going to fall into the sea. He wouldn't let even vague acquaintances drown in their beds.

There was also the creature living in the basement and its waterlogged birdcalls gurgling at all hours of the night. Glen didn't know how it would take to having neighbors.

Glen only had to flash his pistol twice. Most squatters left peacefully once discovered. The first was a pair of heroin addicts shooting up in a second-story unit. The second was a man kneeling on the basement stairs, screaming at the creature below. The thing had grown restless, whipping the standing water into a froth, its three skeletal tails cracking against the sunken steps in abrasive rasps. It nosed out of the water, a collection of mouths and overlapping teeth worrying the air, biting down again and again on its own scaled flesh. Glen had grown protective of the aquatic being, so he was a little more gruff with the man than he had been with the addicts.

As he threw the man, still ranting, into the street, Glen managed to catch the end of his warning, *That monster will be the death of us, mark my words*. And Glen did. He jotted them down in the weekly report his boss continued to ignore.

•

Glen had grown lazy in his search for squatters, preferring to stand at the top of the basement stairs, watching the creature's fins as it gracefully swam about. He'd throw food into the water: hot dogs and bread, chocolate bars and cheese sticks. But the creature never ate, its many mouths remaining shut. When the laughter of children filtered through the ceiling one night, he couldn't make up an excuse not to look, even though he hated evicting families.

Shouldering through the condo's door, he found three kids huddled around an electric lantern, reading knock-knock jokes from a library book in the dim light, the mother making sandwiches from Kraft Singles.

"I'm sorry, but you have to leave," Glen said.

"I know," the mother answered. "Could we just stay the night? The rain's so heavy and there's nowhere to go."

"I want to say yes, but this building's collapsing."

"It won't tonight."

Glenn sighed. "There's also this thing in the basement. I don't know what it eats. You might find it on your doorstep instead of me next time."

"I'm not worried about that. All houses like this have something in the basement, or the attic. Beneath the stairs, under the deck. We've been in enough places to know."

"It's your call. If you promise to be out by morning, I won't call the cops," Glenn said.

"We'll be out before sunrise," the mother replied, resignation tinting her words.

Glenn nodded and walked toward the door. The kids began reading jokes as he slipped around their lantern-lit semicircle. Before stepping into the hall, he turned to the woman. "Do you know what that thing eats? The creature downstairs?"

"I figured it ate whoever lived here first. Why would anyone abandon a house like this otherwise?" the woman said.

"I don't think that's what— " Glen began to say before the woman cut him off.

"No. I'm sure. People don't abandon homes when they actually have them."

Glen nodded, closing the door behind himself. From the woman's wide-eyed look, the way her teeth clenched behind cracked lips, he knew he wouldn't change her mind. The next morning, when he'd come back to check, he hoped he'd find the creature swimming in its usual pool, the condo's walls clean and blood-free, and the children's library books gone from the top floor.

Lifeline

J. S. BREUKELAAR

It was a weeknight, very late, so the club was half empty and the only people Joel kind of knew were behind the bar—he'd dated someone who didn't work there anymore. There were some girls dancing and their loveliness made his eyes water but his need was emotional, not physical, and he knew that about himself, how he must reek of 40-proof loneliness. The girls slowed their dancing when he walked past like they could smell it too. Someone smiled at him from the bar and she was pretty but all he saw in her gray eyes was a reflection of his own need, so he kept on walking.

Above the urinal there was a flyer that looked recently posted, for yet another psychic—a palm reader this time. The club was downstairs in a converted brick factory and according to the flyer, the psychic, whose name was Cherry, was upstairs. Joel thought that Cherry was a good name for a palm reader. CHERRY SLOANE, CHIROLOGIST, the flyer said, and there were some letters after her name. Joel washed his hands and went out to the bar. He ordered a drink he didn't want. He asked the bartender about the palm reader upstairs, and she said she hadn't heard much about her, nothing bad anyway. Joel remembered that his ex had gone to a psychic, and he wondered if that had something to do with them breaking up. When Joel was little, his mother had taken him and his brother to a carnival and they'd put money in a "Chiromancy" machine and a card popped out that told his mother's fortune, and she kept the card as a memento of one of the happiest days of her life.

Joel put down his drink and followed the EXIT signs to some stairs, where a piece of paper with a penciled arrow said, CHERRY'S PLACE. He climbed the stairs, which were wide and pocked, and the music from the club receded to a muffled thud that slowly died, like a heartbeat that stopped. He emerged in a room so dark and vast that he couldn't see the edges. Dirty windows overlooked the street below, the famous smokestacks blurry behind a buildup of silt and dust on the glass. A woman sat bent over a laptop at a table in the far-left corner, the glow of a desk lamp drawing all the light in the room to her face. He heard a whispering but she had her mouth closed. A slouched shadow heaved in a distant corner of the room.

He knew then that he'd made a terrible mistake. But the minute he turned to go, the woman's head snapped up and he froze. She was elderly with thinning white hair. Her face was covered in tattoos and there were tattoos on her hands, too, all the way to where her grimy cardigan covered her wrists. She had webbing between her fingers.

"Lines, ten bucks," she said. "Fifteen for mounts."

Joel wondered what kind of body-mod artist would do this to an old lady. He didn't know what a mount was. He just wanted to get out of there, but those rheumy eyes peering from their mask of ink held him in place. Most of his friends had tattoos, and he had a couple too. A hamburger on the back of one calf, and his ex's initials somewhere he'd forgotten now. The palm reader had the Milky Way tattooed across her throat, the entire solar system below that. He could see Venus from here, glowing malevolently between the missing buttons of her cardigan.

"Just lines," he said. "Don't suppose you take—"

She tapped on a credit card terminal with a long-nailed finger.

Joel sat down opposite her at the desk by the window. A streetlight infused that corner of the room with a pee-colored glow. He could hear the rumble of trucks. He listened for music from the club below but the room was silent, except for the occasional whisper behind him that he must be imagining.

"I can't stay," he said. "Not sure how long this'll take."

"Places to go, people to kill, eh?" She didn't smile, and her voice was phlegmy.

"Just some friends of mine downstairs. They dared me, you know, so."

She'd taken his hand in her webbed ones while he was talking. Her touch gave him a jolt of nausea; spit pooled in his mouth. She turned his hand over, touched the underside of his fingers with hers. "You don't have any friends," she said.

A sound like a book dropping onto the floor made him start but she seemed not to hear it. She eyed him, still with her fingers resting lightly on his, and cradling his wrist delicately in her other hand, her pinky extended so that he could see tiny veins in the webbing.

She placed his hand gently down on her filthy desk—there were tissues stuffed in a teacup—still without looking at it.

"I can't take your money," she said. "Sorry."

Something in that voice said it wasn't the money she was sorry about.

"What?" he said. But he didn't stand up. "Did you see something bad? You didn't look for very long. Not even *at* my palm." He shoved it at her, but she didn't move.

He drew ten dollars from his pocket and slapped it on the table. "What did you see?"

"I'm half blind," she said. "Who am I to—"

"Tell me," he said. "I can take it."

"You have no choice," she said. "None of us do." She swept her arms out across the room, exposing a swirling geography of tattoos on her crepey old-lady arms.

"Tell me," he said.

She slumped in her seat. "The others . . ."

"I don't care about the others."

She pulled a used tissue from a pocket. "None of them do. Or they wouldn't come to me. But that changes too."

"Tell me," he said.

A tear oozed from her eye and began to fall down an impossible staircase inked on her hollow cheek.

"You will die—" she said.

Joel stood up so violently the chair crashed onto the floor. There was a shifting in the air behind him. "Crazy bitch!" he shrieked.

He was almost at the stairs when she said, "—the moment you leave the building." Turning back was the wrong thing to do, but he did it anyway.

"What?" he said. Shapes began to solidify at the edge of his eye. "Your life will end with you walking out of here."

He began to laugh so hard that he started to cry.

It was then that he noticed a pile of pizza boxes on one of the desks. A mattress on the floor—a guy bent cross-legged over a book. There were others, too. All of them around his age, propped against the wall, rolling cigs or murmuring together like they had always been there.

A girl sat on a worn couch, trimming her brown hair with office scissors. "Welcome," she said. She was maybe thirty, thirty-one. She stood up. Gilded hunks of hair floated to the floor. "I'll show you your room."

Jane Death Theory #13

RION AMILCAR SCOTT

I t's possible, Officer Samuel Duncan[1] mused while standing by his squad car with two of his colleagues late one night on the side of an empty road—it's possible for someone to shoot herself while locked in a squad car with metal restraints binding her hands behind her back.

---

1. On November 19, 2013, the Durham, NC, police officer Samuel Duncan took seventeen-year-old Jesus Huerta into custody on a trespassing warrant after his parents called police to report that he had run away. Duncan searched the teen, handcuffed him (with his hands behind his back), and placed him in the back of a cruiser. Before he could make it to the police station, Huerta died from a gunshot wound to his face. Cameras in the cruiser were switched off at the time and did not record the gunshot. Authorities ruled the death of the handcuffed Huerta a suicide. (Source: abc11.com)

His partner, Ron Marsh,[2] became quiet, gazed sadly at the bloody mass in the backseat, and after a moment of thinking, replied, Yes. Let's say she secrets the weapon in the small of her back so it's invisible during a search, and since her hands are back there, she reaches for it. If she jerks her head to the left or to the right she could conceivably angle the gun toward her temple. Sure, Officer Duncan said. Sure. I can see how that, while not probable, could make a kind of sense in the absence of another explanation. Trooper 1st Class Stephen Hammons[3] stood with his arms folded, frowning sternly, a shadow cast from the large brim of his trooper hat darkening his face, almost to the shade of their once-belligerent prisoner, Ron Marsh joked earlier. Trooper Hammons had refused to crack even the hint of a smile. Now he chimed in: And with her dead, she's not able

---

2. In Little Rock, AR, on July 28, 2012, Officer Ron Marsh took twenty-one-year-old Chavis Carter into custody. He frisked Carter—turning up marijuana, but no gun—and placed him in the back of a patrol car. Carter suffered a fatal gunshot wound to the head while handcuffed in the backseat of the cruiser. Authorities ruled Carter's death a suicide. (Source: *The Huffington Post*)

3. In August 2012, state police in New Iberia, LA, searched twenty-two-year-old Victor White III after taking him into custody, discovering only illegal drugs, and placed him in the back of a squad car. While in the squad car, White was shot. He died later from the gunshot wound. According to a Louisiana State Police spokesman, Trooper 1st Class Stephen Hammons, the handcuffed White shot himself in the back with a gun he hid from police during the search. An autopsy done by the Iberia Parish Coroner's Office later determined that White was shot in the chest. Authorities ruled his death a suicide. (Sources: CBSnews.com; *The Advocate*; NewsOne)

to provide any sort of counternarrative. Officer Duncan nodded: Yeah, that sounds possible, doesn't it? Officer Marsh snorted, smoothed his mustache. Who would believe the alternative? he said. It's almost too horrible to conceive, isn't it?

The Blue Room

LENA VALENCIA

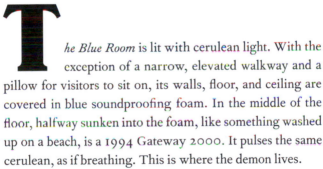

The *Blue Room* is lit with cerulean light. With the exception of a narrow, elevated walkway and a pillow for visitors to sit on, its walls, floor, and ceiling are covered in blue soundproofing foam. In the middle of the floor, halfway sunken into the foam, like something washed up on a beach, is a 1994 Gateway 2000. It pulses the same cerulean, as if breathing. This is where the demon lives.

Fern has been waiting to see *The Blue Room* for two hours. Normally, she's able to cut these lines. Fern is a successful art world influencer. Tens of thousands of followers watch her account. But not even she can convince the gallery assistant to let her get any closer to the latest Josephine Fibonacci installation—the artist's final work. Fibonacci has been declared officially missing as of last Tuesday, causing a stir in the art world. No doubt one reason for the line, which now snakes behind Fern through the streets of Chelsea. Finally, she gets to the front, where a large sign conveys the rules of the exhibition to visitors. *No shoes. No jackets. No bags.* And then: The Blue Room *is a device-free space for contemplation. In order to fully experience the anechoic chamber and the demon that inhabits it, the artist requests that you surrender your electronic devices at the entrance.*

She ungracefully removes her platform combat boots, shoving them into the provided locker along with her purse and phone. She's prepared for this. She's hidden a second phone—her real phone—in the pocket of her billowing silk pants.

There is some debate among critics as to whether the demon is real. Some say it's just a metaphor for our obsession with screens, an illusion. But others have reported feeling an unexplained static electricity clinging to their skin after leaving the installation. Everyone wants to see for themselves, which is why Fern feels compelled to do what no one has yet done: capture the demon on video.

Fern enters *The Blue Room*. She sits on the pillow, positioning her body so that the security guard can't see her midsection, and pulls out her phone, slouching awkwardly to conceal it. She starts filming. For the first few minutes, there's nothing but the blue pulsing. It's silent. Fern hears her stomach gurgle, her breath, her heartbeat, and feels a profound reverence for the miracle that is the human body. The whisper-hum of the computer's fan grows louder.

The demon takes shape on the screen. It's a woman,

face and body blurred. It steps out of the screen and grows larger, until it towers over Fern. It's wearing a long white dress, its yellow-green hair blowing around its face, though there is no wind. Fern gasps. The demon opens her mouth to speak, but its voice is obscured by the computer's fan, now loud as a train barreling through the room. Somewhere she smells burning plastic. The demon begins to twirl. Fern grows dizzy watching it. She puts a hand on the floor to right herself.

A chime goes off. The demon disappears in a flash of blue. Fern's time is up. She stands, concealing her phone in her pants, and shakily exits the room.

Outside, Fern watches the video she's taken. On the phone, the demon looks unremarkable: vapor, a puff of steam, but on closer inspection she can still make out the face, the dress. Her ears ring. She's lightheaded. Perhaps this is the effect of true genius. Her phone seems to grow heavy in her hand. She realizes she's late for drinks with her friend Amir.

Amir is drunk by the time she arrives at the bar. He thinks that *The Blue Room* is totally derivative, though he admits he hasn't seen it. An artist himself, he's into more transgressive stuff, she knows—Fibonacci is too tame for him. Still, she tries to explain her experience. The words come out as platitudes: the energy of the room, the stillness of it. Amir doesn't seem to care.

This will be the last time anyone sees Fern in person.

•

Back home, Fern posts videos about her day: selfies in line for the installation; Amir drinking; a stencil reading "Never give up on beauty" on the sidewalk; the demon. Views and messages begin to roll in. Then, without warning, her phone dies right there in her hand. She groans and plugs it into the wall to charge.

Fern tells people that she's able to fully support herself through the endorsements she gets on Instagram, but the truth is her brother Ricardo, who works at a hedge fund, pays the rent and the phone bill. The endorsements can pay for groceries on a good week. Mostly the companies just send her free clothes and jewelry to wear and post about.

She lives in a loft above a steakhouse with a roommate who is never home. The aroma that lingers in the air shaft means Fern is always hungry for meat, though she's been vegan for years now. She's spooning leftover takeout rice into her mouth when she hears a moan. She peeks out the kitchen window, expecting to see a cat in heat. All that's there is a cook having a cigarette.

On her bed, the phone has switched on again. It's frozen on a light blue screen. Fern realizes with a little shiver that it's the same color as the Fibonacci installation. Then the moaning starts again.

It's coming from the phone. She tries to turn it off, pressing the power button repeatedly, but the blue remains. She flings it onto the hardwood floor. This doesn't do any good either. A minuscule crack has formed in the screen. Smoke curls from beneath the glass. Soon all Fern can smell is frying steak and the burning plastic from the installation. She gags.

The vertigo sweeps over her and all she can see is blue.

For the second Thursday night in a row, Fern isn't at the gallery openings, which is unusual. Amir has wandered through of all of them, refilling a disposable plastic cup with bourbon from his flask. It feels weird to be here without Fern. Her Instagram has changed. It's video after video of her twirling around in endless circles. Or is it her? It seems the longer he looks, the more her features alter. When he texts, her replies are cryptic: Blue heart emojis. Strings of meaningless words.

An arm creeps around his waist and he jumps. It's Bella Thayer, the art critic, drunk.

"Amir!" she exclaims, shoving a strand of platinum hair away from her face. "Can you explain this pretentious crap to me?" On her phone is a tiny twirling Fern. They watch together.

"I can't," he mutters. He's cold all of a sudden, though the gallery is stifling.

"Should we ditch the scene and go somewhere?" says Bella. They are still watching Fern spin, the same panicked look on her face each time it meets the camera.

"Please," says Amir. Bella puts her phone away. Arm in arm, the two of them push their way through the crowd to meet the night.

Unbeknownst

MATTHEW VOLLMER

The man woke from a dream in which he and his son had been to a movie and during intermission they had gone outside to see the fireworks but it had been snowing so hard that the rockets tossed by a man for a crowd of gawkers sputtered and died and to get back to the theater they had to follow a trail that passed by some hot springs—the kind you'd see in Yellowstone—and the man had lost sight of his son and turned down a path of sticky ground, which he realized too late was the tongue of a carnivorous plant whose stamen was a purplish brainlike thing and whose leaves, in an act of sinister entrapment, folded over and enclosed him.

That's when he woke up.

The clock read 5:59. He thought about getting up. He'd been telling himself he should get up early, that sleeping until 6:30 or 7:00 or even 7:40 on one recent occasion was irresponsible if not downright slothful and that soon the sun would be up, warming the earth, and because it was summer, it would soon be too hot to comfortably exercise out of doors, which he needed desperately to do. *One more minute*, he thought.

He would've drifted off again except that this time he began to snore just before he lost consciousness. He opened his eyes. Checked the clock: 5:59. This particular minute, apparently, was longer than usual. The entrance into the realm of not-quite-awake-slash-not-quite-asleep had allowed him to misperceive time, maybe. No big deal. He stared down the clock. As soon as it hit 6:00, he told himself, he'd slide out of bed. He'd walk quietly across the bedroom floor so as not to wake his wife, step into the hallway, close his son's door, let the dog out to pee.

5:59.

He counted down from ten to one, a little thing he did sometimes when waiting for numbers on a clock to change or anticipating a traffic light switching from red to green, enjoying the momentary illusion that he had even a modicum of power over the world and the things in it, that simply by thought control he could enact transformations upon things that were otherwise autonomous or, at the very least, programmed to give that impression.

5:59.

He repeated the countdown.

The clock remained unchanged.

He glanced toward the window. The light—a paleness that signaled a summer sunrise—was believably 5:59-ish. Back to the clock.

5:59.

He repeated his countdown thrice more, but only to make it absolutely certain in his mind: the clock was stuck. Maybe, he thought, it had malfunctioned. He'd seen plenty of stopped clocks, but they'd all been analog. This thing, despite being digital, was old. It'd been a wedding present, probably appeared on a gift registry, back when he and his wife had toured a store that specialized in domestic merchandise, carrying a little gun they fired at the UPCs of items they wanted, so as to create their own personalized wish list, an event that had seemed to both of them like the closest they'd ever come to a shopping spree. When he really thought about it, he had to admit that it was kind of amazing, what with the planned obsolescence of all things digital, that such a clock had lasted as long as it had. Back in their old duplex—the first place they'd ever lived together, right after they'd gotten married—they'd left a bedside lamp on too long, its head positioned (who knows why) only inches above the snooze button, and the resultant heat had melted the plastic, warping the button and merging it with the clock body, thus rendering it impossible to delay the inevitable, not that either he or his wife were ever the kind of people to punch a snooze button.

He slid on a pair of blue shorts with an elastic waistband and three stripes down the sides. In the kitchen, the oven and microwave clocks both read 5:57. As they had never been synchronized with the bedroom clock, which magically set itself once a user plugged it in, they had remained, since the last power outage, two minutes behind, like the watch that the man wore. The watch, as its battery had died a couple of days ago, and had not been replaced due, in part, to procrastination, and in part to the man having visited the one jewelry store he knew in town and finding it closed, showed no numbers at all.

The man performed the countdown again. And again. Each time, the act only emphasized his powerlessness. He went downstairs to his office, which was on the lower floor of the house, and to get there he had to cross an unfinished storage room, which was vast and windowless and dark. He flicked the light switch but remembered that both bulbs had burned out and that for some reason, when he'd attempted to replace them, the new bulbs hadn't worked. He'd been meaning to call an electrician. *Today*, he thought, as he had for over a week now.

He wiggled the computer mouse. The screen failed to brighten. He tapped on the keyboard. Nada. He unhooked his smartphone, pressed its power button. Nothing changed.

Back upstairs, he nudged his wife. Said her name. She didn't respond. He grabbed her wrist. Thought, at first, that he felt a pulse, but couldn't be sure that it wasn't his own heartbeat in his fingertips. Still, she was warm. He peeled back her eyelids. He yelled into her ear.

Nothing.

He picked up the landline, which his wife insisted they continue to pay for, in case of emergencies. This seemed like it might be one, but there was no dial tone. Outside, on the porch: no breeze. The trees didn't move. The traffic light in the distance appeared to be stuck on red. No cars appeared on the road.

He crawled back into bed. What else was there to do but wait? He had a bad feeling, like this wasn't the kind of dream he could stop by making himself fall asleep inside it. He turned over, faced the wall, and pledged that he wouldn't open his eyes until he heard a sound: the dog's collar shaking, the squeak of the wooden ladder as his son descended his bunk, the rustle of covers as his wife finally woke. And then, and only then, he would make a sound of his own, a kind of whine or grunt to protest the fact that she'd gotten up without hugging him first, a sound that his wife, who knew him better than anyone else in the world, would knowingly interpret and most likely indulge, by hugging him before she got dressed. Yes, he told himself. He could wait, and he would, for however long it took, not knowing, even now, as he was drifting into the dark, imagining his wife's hand on his face, that she was trying, without success, to shake him awake.

Lone

JAC JEMC

Adrienne woke feeling rested, a surprise after a night camping by herself. She had survived unharmed, with nothing between her and the wilderness but a thin sheet of nylon.

She committed herself to making it work. She had lost so much since breaking up with Sam and refused to add camping to the list of casualties.

The couples they'd camped with before were hesitant to commit to a three-person weekend getaway with her. Even the ones who sided more with her seemed to be perennially booked. She asked individual friends to come along, but they all had reasons to say no. Jaclyn insisted she hated roughing it despite Adrienne's attempts to convince her she had all the gear to make it luxurious—a huge tent, air mattresses, a propane stove to make coffee in the morning easy, and a veritable tank of bourbon. Parra had read a book that didn't end well about women camping alone together. Mal kept committing and then backing out. Adrienne finally broke down and decided to go solo.

She'd already booked her site at Summit Lake. She reviewed her Tupperware tote of supplies and added a roll of paper towels and a new bottle of bug spray. She went to the grocery store the day before and chopped vegetables and kneaded hamburger patties and packed everything into the cooler.

To others, she wanted to appear strong, hiding any clues of vulnerability to encourage them to accompany her, but she was incensed that she did have nerves about camping alone. How dare she be deprived of this? How dare she be kept from a night closer to nature, hearing all those sounds and smelling those smells and feeling just slightly more like an animal who existed in a real, live world. It rejuvenated her. It powered her back up for work and the other mundanities required of her.

Only one thing sparked the fear: men. Bears or raccoons or spiders did not intimidate her. In fact, Adrienne often thought, she'd be happiest if her death came in the form of an animal attack: a survival of the fittest that she couldn't disagree with. She could not stand, however, the idea of a man harming her in the woods. She took issue with the way it would so inaccurately reflect the balance of power, the level of need and security of the parties involved.

She had given so much to Sam just to get him to go, just

to be sure he would be okay without her, and still she felt people's pity when she shared the news of the breakup, as though she were the victim, when, in fact, she had been in charge. He was the one who untagged her from all his photos on social media, unable to deal with the painful memories. He was the one who had unfriended her after she asked him to leave. She flared at the thought.

When she saw the pair of old hiking boots Sam had left behind in the basement, her first thought was to throw them away. Her second thought was to call him and tell him she'd left them on the front porch for him to pick up, eliminating any need for interaction. But that gave her an idea. She thought of how, after her grandfather died, her grandmother left all the bills in his name, so that if people looked at her mail, they wouldn't know she lived alone. If Adrienne took the boots with her, and placed them outside the tent, anyone passing by would assume a man slept inside. If a human predator were looking for innocent prey, they'd think twice.

The night before, she'd set up her tent first and built her fire second. She loved getting the fire going, had always made it her task, even when Sam pretended mastery in the company of friends. She poured herself a bourbon in a tin cup, set out her food on the grate and tended it with care. The sun had set by the time the meat had cooked through. She added logs to the heap and set marshmallows on fire. She took a selfie lit by the flames. She videoed the ooze of a s'more. She took a photo of the sky, disappointed at the dimness of the stars as they appeared on her phone's screen. She had no service out here, but she would show off her solo camping skills on Sunday when she returned to civilization.

Her site was near the latrine, and she watched as other campers made their final trips before settling in for the night. By the pairs of people and conversations overheard, she determined the campground to be occupied by couples and families.

She wondered if she was being paranoid, but, in the end, when the fire had withered, she set the boots outside the tent and zipped herself in. She read a magazine by lantern light on her air mattress with a final finger of liquor, popped a ZzzQuil, and fell asleep.

In the morning, she made coffee. She loved the dewy chill, how her nose felt both runny and clear. She tugged her hat down over her ears and cradled her mug close as she watched people pass on their morning trips to the latrine. A man waved at her, and Adrienne failed to decipher something in his expression. His smile held some sort of secret. She waited for him to walk back past her, but she didn't see him again. Maybe he'd gone out for a hike, or he'd walked back to his site a different way. She thought about what she wanted to do that day, but couldn't get the man's smile out of her head.

She'd booked the site for two nights, but she packed the tent up. She threw the tub of supplies and the cooler back into the car. She decided to leave the boots right where they were. Sam would buy a new pair, and Adrienne wouldn't need them again. Something had changed and, despite the peaceful night, she knew she wouldn't be camping alone again.

She made the two-hour drive crying, furious with herself.

At home she transferred everything from the cooler to the fridge. She threw her bedding in the wash with shaking hands. She poured herself a drink to calm herself down and took out her phone to post the photos with a caption that painted the overnight in the positive light she'd counted on. She opened her photos and understood.

She saw the selfie in front of the fire and the video of the s'more. She remembered trying to capture the stars.

But she saw three more photos she hadn't taken herself: the boots outside the tent in the dark, her sleeping body inside, and then a close-up of the bottom half of a man's face, grinning.

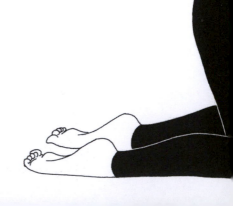

Smoldering Pipeworks. My mother and I were living with a woman named Susan whom my mom had known since high school. Susan lived in a small one-bedroom trailer in the next town over from mine. She had a two-and-a-half-year-old son, and she was an alcoholic, as was my mother, but Susan was sloppier about it than my mom. She was a very violent and argumentative drunk.

In her one-bedroom trailer, Susan had a queen-size bed boasting an ornate metal headboard and frame. When she got drunk and started arguing with the people she often had over for drinking and arguing, I would go into the bedroom, crawl up in the bed, cover one ear, and press the other against the metal headboard. By pressing my ear against the metal poles, I could hear it. The sonorous metal poles produced a mournful and straining racket that sounded like a combination of an old ironworker's shop and a torture chamber.

The fairy-tale movie *Legend*, which I loved, included many scenes depicting an upper level of Hell where trolls and demons lived in a nightmarish factory just below the earth, where they were constantly hammering metal and grinding steel and burning coal and torturing the creatures they caught and dragged down and imprisoned in their metal cages. I thought I was hearing this sort of thing—that in some supernatural dimension, the poles of Susan's bedframe led all the way down to a horrible, mythical pit in the earth, some deep, smoldering Pipeworks, where weapons were being forged from flame and iron, and people were

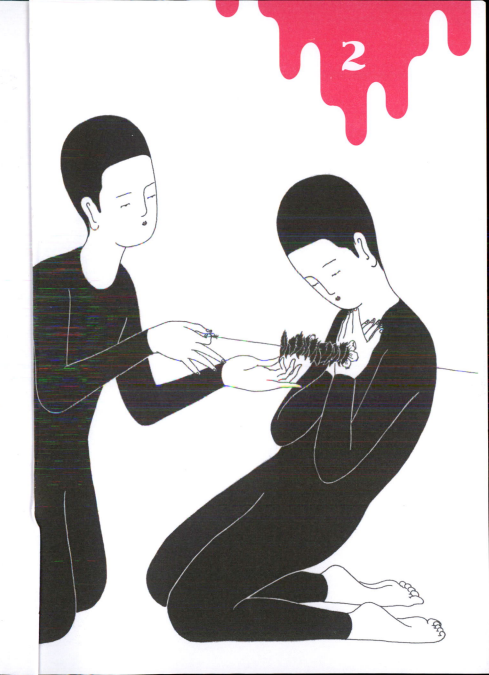

Pipeworks

CHAVISA WOODS

Sometimes, trees look like men. In the dim
of dusk when they sway in the wind, from
tance, the white trees especially stand out against the
edge. They appear to be a slim man watching and waitin
something unknown so that he can begin his brutal wor

When I was very young, I used to see things that no
else saw. One of the things I saw often was a faceless
with a head of bushy white hair. He watched me thro
windows. I thought he was a real man following me arou
just to stare and disappear.

I saw many things that other people didn't see. I
heard things that other people didn't hear, and sometin
I heard things that other people did hear, but I interpre
them very differently than others would have.

I was five years old when I discovered the D

being raped and burned and pulled apart limb by limb, skinned alive; boiled in giant metal cauldrons, and branded with Satan's irons.

One night, when I was staying with my mother, Susan went out to the bars with some friends of hers, and my mother and I stayed home to babysit Susan's two-and-a-half-year-old son. We had a nice time that evening, passing many hours playing games and eating snacks.

My mother, myself, and Susan's young son were sitting on the floor of the trailer, and Susan came in slurring and wobbling and talking loudly. She smiled at us and asked if we'd had a good time, then sat in a chair near me, and held her arms open to her baby boy. "Come here," she said, "give Mommy a hug." The boy squealed and threw his hands out, laughing, and ran, not to her, but to my mother, Gina. He crawled into my mom's lap and turned back to his mom. "No!" he squealed, still giggling, "Gina!" Then he hid his face in my mother's chest, and laughed like a cartoon baby who was being ornery. He was obviously trying to play, but Susan's response was brutal. Her expression dropped suddenly. Her eyes became dark. Her mouth, a stiff line.

"You love *her* more than me?" she asked, not playing in any way. "You want her to be your mom now? Is that it?"

She grabbed him out of my mom's lap and sat him in the middle of the floor. The boy began crying. My mom told her to calm down. "You're just drunk. He knows you're his momma. We've just been having fun, that's all," she pleaded.

She walked around and sat on the floor across from my mom, with her son sitting in between them. She looked at that two-and-a-half-year-old boy who still wobbled when he walked, and she told him, "You're gonna have to choose. You want to go to me or her? You fucking choose who you love more. You hear me? You go to who you love more!"

"Susan, stop it. This is sick," my mom demanded.

I crawled up onto the chair and curled my knees to my chest.

"You better choose right, *boy*," she told him menacingly. "Now, call him." My mom sighed deeply and a sorrowful look took over her face. She shook her head and remained silent. "Come here!" Susan shouted. "You better get over here, boy! Come to your fucking momma!" Susan was screaming at this point, so, of course, the child was terrified, and even though she wasn't even calling him, he went as fast as he could back into my mother's arms.

And then Susan stood, grabbed the toddler by his arm, and gave him three very hard smacks in the face. My mother screamed at her and reached for the boy, but Susan quickly grabbed him by his hair and began dragging him out of the living room and down the hall toward the bedroom, as he screamed for his life.

I can still see him. It's like a short video that goes in a loop whenever I think of it. I can see his face twisted up in anguish, his feet barely touching the ground, facing me with his hair tangled in his mother's fist, as she dragged him behind her down the brown-carpeted hallway so she could lock herself in the bedroom with him and beat him all she liked, until he "learned to love her more."

My mom leaped to her feet, sprinted down the hallway, and got to Susan before she reached the bedroom. They began scuffling and my mother beat Susan back into the living room with a series of shoves and punches, taking a couple of hard smacks to the face herself. The boy was left in the hallway, crying.

"Calm the fuck down!" my mom screamed at Susan as she shoved her so hard that she toppled backward, landing on the couch. My mother turned, scooped me up, and took off running down the hallway with me. Susan got up from the couch and came after us, shouting curses as she came. My mom let me down and told me to run to the bedroom, so she could scoop up Susan's young son. "Run, Sissy, run!" she shouted as she ran fast behind me with the boy in her arms. We made it into the bedroom and my mom slammed the door closed just as Susan landed on it and began slamming her full body into it. "He's *my* son, you bitch," Susan screamed. "I'll kill you, you little bitch. I'll fucking kill you when I get my hands on you." She kept pounding on the door and screaming about the horrible things she wanted to do to us.

Mom got on the bed with us and took the boy. I curled up beside her, against the bedframe, covered one ear with the palm of my hand, and pressed my other ear to the paranormal metal headboard. I heard a man lift a hammer and bring it down, and someone wail, as a machine creaked out its ghastly work. I heard people pounding on the walls to be let out of the dungeons, and imagined what crimes they were being punished for, and who would escape, and who would perish in the flames of coal fire. I heard a young couple whispering their final goodbyes, as the wooden racks they were tied to were lifted and poured into the pit of flame, and reveled in the creek and pop of the metal and wood and flesh and bone as it was eaten by the fire. I stayed there like that, curled next to my mother, my ear pressed against the bedpost, drowning out Susan's screaming and threatening with the entrancing and oddly comforting sounds of that subterranean torture chamber.

The Owner

WHITNEY COLLINS

Nina and her husband, Harry, got a good deal on the house. It was a charming, bone-colored Cape Cod that seemed to have an agreement with the elements. All over, it was tilted and weathered but also sturdy—petrified almost. They never met the owner. "He's in Florida now," the Realtor said, unprompted, twice during the closing. She said it in a plain, firm way that Nina and her husband did not question. She said it like Florida meant Mars or Hell.

On the first night in the house, Nina dreamed of the owner. He sat in a canvas chair in the desert. To his left was a stunted palm tree. To his right, a beach ball that didn't roll away. He gazed out over an expanse of red sand. He wore a gas mask, but Nina could still hear what he said. "I left you something. Did you find it?"

Nina woke with a jolt. Beside her, Harry breathed serenely. She rose and went into the bathroom and opened the medicine cabinet. She wanted an aspirin, but all she found was a Band-Aid tin—the vintage, metal kind—and inside of that, a single white bead. Nina inspected the bead. It was the size of a large pea with a tidy, drilled hole. She put the bead back into the tin and the tin back into the cabinet. She drank from the faucet. When she returned to bed, she could not sleep. She kept seeing the gas mask, the stunted palm. She kept trying to move the beach ball with her thoughts.

In the morning, while Nina stood in front of the toaster, Harry came up behind her and kissed the nape of her neck. When she turned around, he wasn't there. "Harry?" she called. "Was that you?" Harry didn't answer, even when she called out again. Nina stood, frowning, until her toast popped up. In that short time, to her surprise, she was able to recall every argument she and Harry had ever had. There had been problems with money and romance, fertility and drinking. Right after they'd first married, there'd also been a woman. A neighbor named Pearl who visited three or four times a week with something from her garden: profane-looking cucumbers, swollen purple tomatoes, fistfuls of fragrant basil. She was good-natured about everything and everyone. There was always a ladybug in her hair. Nina had never seen Harry so happy. He accepted everything Pearl brought without once looking down at what Pearl brought. "You look at her too much," Nina had said. "Maybe you could learn a thing or two," Harry had said back.

Nina hadn't thought of Pearl in a long time. She was filled with a sudden sadness. She left the toast in the toaster to grow stale. She went back to the bedroom and curled on the bed. This time, when she dreamed of the owner, he had two gas masks—one on his face and one that he held out for Nina. The beach ball was still in the same place. The palm tree was nearly dead. When Nina woke up, she discovered two more white beads on the floor, side by side.

Every day, in an unexpected place, Nina found another bead. She found one in the lint screen of the dryer. One in the soil of a cactus she repotted. One at the bottom of a bowl of tomato soup. One day, she coughed a single cough and a bead appeared on her tongue. Nina kept all the beads. She stored them in the Band-Aid tin. Sometimes she shook the tin to hear the noise it made. *Gotcha, gotcha, gotcha*, it said.

Nina and Harry weren't happy in the new house; they bickered all the time. The only thing that brought Nina hope were the beads and the dreams, though neither of those made any real sense to her. She slept excessively. Harry came home later and later in the evenings smelling of beer, cigars, perfume. When he slept, he no longer breathed serenely. Instead, he snored, causing Nina's dreams to take an urgent turn. There was a loud, new factory in the desert, churning out clouds of navy smoke, and she and the owner would sit in his canvas chairs wearing gas masks looking at it.

"What are they making?" she'd ask him.

"It's not what you think," he'd say.

Then Nina would wake up and drink from the faucet and discover another bead. Maybe pressed into the soft, pink meat of her heel. Maybe near the sink drain, in the tiny groove that kept it from drowning.

When Nina had forty beads, she spread them on the kitchen table after Harry had gone to work. She put twenty in one row, then twenty in a row below it. She pretended they were teeth. While she arranged the beads, someone came and kissed her on the nape of her neck, but this time she did not turn to see who it was. That night, Harry was the latest he had ever been.

"Where have you been?" Nina asked.

"It's not what you think," he said.

Harry swayed at the foot of the bed. Nina felt her hands begin to shake. "I don't like this house," she said. "I wish we'd never bought it."

Harry shook his head. "I knew this would happen."

Nina's eyes filled with tears. She lay back in bed. She heard Harry leave the room and then the house. Then she let herself cry until she was there, in the desert with the owner, reaching out for the gas mask and putting it on.

"What happened to the palm tree?" Nina asked.

"It died," said the owner.

"And the beach ball?"

"It rolled away."

Nina didn't want to sit in the canvas chair. "Let's walk to the factory," she said. "Let's see what they make."

The owner said nothing, but he got up and off they went, across the red sand together. The factory was larger and louder than life and made of black glass. When they got up to it, Nina pressed her face against it but couldn't see inside. All she could see was her own reflection, her face in its gas mask, and the owner standing behind her, his face in his.

"Look what I have," he said. He held up something small and square and gave it a shake. *Gotcha, gotcha, gotcha.* Nina froze, petrified. She watched as the owner opened the tin and brought out the beads. All forty were now on a string, and he placed them around her neck, stopping to kiss her nape, before he fastened them. Nina placed one palm on the factory's black glass, the other at the hollow of her throat. As the necklace grew tighter, the factory grew louder. She thought to call for Harry, but she could not speak, could not breathe. She could only see the image of her masked face and that of the owner's looking back at her. Her vision began to dim but not before she saw: a final bead—a red one—on the lens of the owner's mask. Moving, gently. A ladybug.

The Resplendence of Disappearing

IVÁN PARRA GARCIA

TRANSLATED BY ALLANA C. NOYES

He pulled the wooden church door shut and looked up to the sky. Those black birds were still at it, flying circles around the sun in an orderly fashion, with a precision even, never losing the measured distance between themselves. It'd been more than three weeks since they showed up, and still no one knew where they came from, what they wanted, where they were going. He'd spent all day in the church's doorway, watching them through his solar-filtered telescope.

He started off on the dirt road toward town, the

afternoon sun beating down on the half-naked crown of his head as he walked ponderously, his shoulders stiff as bricks under his white shirt, collar unbuttoned. He ruminated on the lack of rain these last few months, about the news, the suffocating September heat, but mostly he thought about the birds.

As he walked along the highway, he turned back to look at the church. For the first time in his fifty years serving Christ, there was doubt in his heart. As if something more powerful than God Himself had come to stay in Texarkana.

He walked on, wishing he were at home in his rocking chair. The diabetes had left his heels cracked and covered in blisters, and his feet were aflame. Hip to toe his legs ached. The doctor had forbidden him from extended periods of standing, but he hadn't paid him any mind.

Stopping in front of a plot of land, he looked northerly through the barbed wire where a coyote was stalking a young deer just a few meters from where he stood. He wiped the sweat from his forehead with the back of his hand, licked his lips, and with a quick slap, obliterated a mosquito on his neck. Lifting the barbed wire, he crossed to the other side one leg at a time. From there he watched the coyote's eyes track the unsuspecting deer, which stood still as a statue, hidden among the dry branches. He lifted a rock and with the little strength he had threw it toward the predator. The rock thumped in the grass and the deer shot off running, while the startled coyote panicked, scampering away through the bramble.

Reverend Vargas trudged through the field. In twenty minutes, he found the dirt road again and walked on it the rest of the way to town.

He stopped in the doorway of José Peloponeso's cigarette shop, where José's daughter was sitting on a white plastic chair with the Friday paper's crossword and a mango Popsicle. She was thirty, with a dark complexion, broad shoulders, and deep, coal-black eyes.

"You see them flying lately?" asked Reverend Vargas, gesturing up toward the firmament. "They look different, like something else."

Milena gnawed at the Popsicle as it began to melt.

"They're just birds, Reverend," she answered, with the crossword splayed across her lap, Popsicle in one hand, pencil in the other. She seemed annoyed.

"Something strange about it. I've kept my eye on them all day. Sometimes seems like the light bounces off them like a mirror. As if they're flying closer to the sun than they are to us."

Milena looked at him, confused and incredulous, then surprised.

"If they were flying close to the sun, they would've burned up." She slurped at the Popsicle.

"You have Pepsi?"

Milena rose, leaving the paper on her chair. She went into the store and came back with a can. He began to speak again as she handed it to him.

"You believe there's such things as nonhuman forces?"

he continued, his gaze fixed on the sky, one hand cupping his forehead to shield his eyes from the light.

"You mean God?"

"No."

This time Milena looked at him suspiciously, wearily, as if trying to decide whether he was putting her faith to the test. He went on:

"All the ones who disappeared these last few weeks came back traumatized. But none can say where they went, why they disappeared, never mind why they keep offing themselves once they're back."

"The police—"

"The police haven't found a thing, not one clue," the reverend interrupted. "Look"—he pointed—"it's like they're from another world. Flying without flapping their wings, they look like perfect triangles, silver-coated, as if they were made of titanium or tin.

Milena sat down again, focusing her attention on the crossword.

Reverend Vargas cracked open his Pepsi and turned to look across the street. A boy, maybe six years old, blew bubbles with a soapy wand in the shade of a nearby building. He looked up the street, down the street. A group of people gathered in front of the Bienestar Bank were talking about it too. One of them held the paper while the others read over his shoulder. They were arguing, as if they couldn't come to a conclusion about what it meant. One man with a long goatee looked up at the sky. A couple who couldn't have been more than twenty years old apiece looked over at the reverend, a flicker of hope in their eyes.

"I wish I could help," he murmured, "but this is out of God's hands."

"Heron! Finally," Milena shouted, scrawling in the last word. "You say something, Reverend?"

But he'd already walked out of the store, continuing down the main road.

On his way back, not far from home, he was walking along the scrub-brush-covered train tracks when he heard a noise that seemed to come from underground. He paused, looking up and down the tracks, but saw only one abandoned coal car. The sound was coming from behind it, a sharp, high-pitched yip, like a chirp. He approached the car, and amid the brush he spotted a brownish yellow cat, curled up into a tight ball of fur. As he bent down to pet it, he saw the deep wound carved into its right flank. Blood was pouring out. Placing two fingers behind its front leg, he felt for its heartbeat, which was slow and deep. It could barely breathe. On the ground next to it lay a bloody pocketknife, an empty bottle of whiskey, a pack of smokes. The reverend looked up and saw two drunks fleeing down the tracks. He yelled after them, but they didn't stop. He felt as if he wanted to chase them, but didn't. Instead, he scooped up the cat, cradling it against his chest as he carried it home.

By the time he arrived, the cat was gasping for air, meowing mournfully. A chill seemed to emanate from its skin. He quickly pushed open the door with his shoulder and set the animal down on his armchair. He filled a dish with water and set it down in front of the cat, but it wouldn't lift its head. Heading back to the kitchen, he flipped on the TV, listening distractedly to the news for a moment before rushing to the bathroom for gauze and Merthiolate, then back to the living room. He crouched in front of the animal, soaking the gauze and dabbing it on the wound. The cat let out a muffled meow. He went back to the kitchen and stood watching the Channel Four news: another disappearance last week, back on Friday night, self-inflicted death Sunday morning.

Leaning both hands on the edge of the sink, he observed the world through the window. The sun had fallen in the sky and glowed reddish against the earth. He knew those birds weren't birds. They weren't of this world. They were something much more powerful, something not even his faith could explain. He watched as a car sped down the road, leaving a cloud of dust behind it, abandoning Texarkana. The cat's labored meowing punctuated the overwhelming silence. He ran back to the living room and saw the awful hemorrhage that spread over the animal's body. In his more than fifty years of existence, he'd seen men and women cross that dark threshold into emptiness, oblivion. A bolt of lightning slick as ice ran through his heart; he could feel it growing, the fulminating hatred for those people he'd seen on the tracks.

Reverend Vargas carried the inert feline body to the

field in front of his house, tenderly placing it next to the garden. Returning to the porch, he slipped off his shoes and sat in the wicker rocker, contemplating the end of yet another day.

The Wheat Woman

THERESA HOTTEL

Graham County, Oklahoma, 1998

As the noon light bounces brilliantly off the kitchen tile and outside the tractor roars —it's summertime, *it never stops*—this mother stares at her daughter and feels an almost violent distance. She feels cold. She feels that her ten-year-old daughter, fidgeting by the dishwasher, is a small, dangerous animal that sneaks through the farmhouse and plans secret attacks. Her daughter looks unkind and white.

Fields surround them. I have to feed this child, the mother thinks. When her back is turned she feels her daughter's eyes slice at her back, unbearable. She senses threat, sourceless and unprecedented: Why? Is it this house? Has her daughter made it so tense? Who is her daughter? Who knows the child's thoughts?

I am a bad mother, the mother thinks. I failed to buy bread. She microwaves a leftover hamburger patty and hesitates. But her daughter's eyes glint and she says she will eat it, plain, wrapped in a napkin. No, she doesn't want rice.

This daughter wants to vomit. She feels it too, a tension like each kitchen surface hides a needle. The tension has built for weeks but unexpectedly unfurled this morning, and now this farmhouse, their home, feels like hands around her throat. She longs to run.

"No," she says again, so the mother shuts the rice cooker. The mother decides to eat like her daughter, chewing meat out of a napkin. They stand at the table, across from each other, sucking up crumbs from the blue paper. Out of loyalty and deep love they both stay. But they don't understand the feeling all around them. Their eyes are cold. They look out the window on the farm. This beautiful American farm. Who are we?

The wheat woman is coming across the field.

The daughter sees this specter from the kitchen window. Slow stroll toward the farmhouse, bare feet curdling soil with each step. She makes a sound like worms within her throat. She might have *flaxen* hair, the daughter thinks, a word learned from an English storybook. "What color is flaxen?" she asks, knowing her mother cannot answer. The mother cannot read English text. When the mother looks out the window she cannot see the wheat woman, she sees only the slow tractor of her American husband, green beast wading through gold crop, back and forth before the window like a parade of provision.

My daughter is a small woman, the mother thinks. I

built a frame for us. I came to this life to escape but I feel hunted, when I should feel at rest.

The daughter can't breathe. Guilt seems to compact her, for no reason. She feels like she has hurt her mother, but her mother before her is unharmed and neither of them can trace the pressure to its source of shame. The wheat woman walks closer.

"Mama," the girl says finally. "I have to tell you. There is a pale woman coming now, across the fields. She is coming here to kill you and take your place in our home. She is beautiful with flaxen hair."

Who is my daughter? What is my daughter? The mother sets her meat-filled napkin down. She feels, incredibly, that the child really wants to hurt her. She feels her daughter's words and eyes like knives, aimed at her exposed neck.

So this is the feeling that makes the house so tense. All this time, that wheat woman drew near.

"Do you love Dad?" the girl wants to know. She forces meat down her throat. She longs to sprint outside and burrow into wheat. Instead she waits. She repeats the question in two languages.

"We're not from here," the mother finally says. "I'm not. It's this place that's wrong for us."

"The wheat is wrong?"

"Wheat fields."

"They're the only fields I've ever known."

She has arrived.

The wheat woman is stooping at their doorway. The wheat woman wants to come inside. She's silhouetted, flaxen, soft, and solid. The mother still cannot see her, but she can smell her, the rich smell of smoked meat, warm lumber.

It's a tender smell. Her daughter looks pinched and vulnerable in the midday light. Her daughter stares at the opening door. Her daughter yearns for the relief she might find.

"Come here," the mother says to her daughter. She opens her arms. "Please, come to me. Don't welcome her."

They wait to see if the daughter will come. In the daughter's sight the wheat woman's mouth cracks open. The wheat woman says, "I love him so." Meanwhile, the mother feels wordless. She has short black hair, speaks English with an unrelenting accent, and her husband calls her his Suzie Wong. She understands the ghost her daughter sees. She knows the hunted, panicked feeling, the need to run to wheat, to make it end. To burrow your body in the surfaces of this land.

"Mama?"

"I can't rest. That's this feeling."

"Where are we from, then? Tell me."

"I can't. There's no place now."

The small, mean-faced daughter backs away from the table. Through the open door, wheat rustles as if alive. The air is humid and heavy. The tractor's hum recedes, then nears, then falls again.

"Welcome me," the wheat woman says. "Welcome rest."

Her words twine with the tractor's hum. The wheat is high and whispering. The daughter longs to let her in. She could let her mother go and thus be free of her mother's burdens, of feelings that smear her own sense of self. The house as tense and sharp and twisted as barbed wire. She grasps the feeling close. She lets it cut her.

Then she turns her back on the door and takes her mother's hand. The mother's fingers are cold and hard as bone. "I can't rest either. I can't breathe. I'll stay with you. I remember."

Like fireworks, the wheat woman screams. Outside, the man leans from his tractor and yells to his wife, and to his daughter, of promises and possession. "Take pity," the wheat woman sobs. "In your denial, I will die." But mother and daughter turn their backs, they have no pity. They must be small and mean and sly and hunted. They know the wheat wants to consume. And so they dig.

Above their heads, the tractor roars.

Harold

SELENA GAMBRELL ANDERSON

Margo Childress had only one father, a tragedy, but he'd built a library with comfortable, modern furniture and double doors that locked, absolutely, from the inside. Opposite the doors stood a high wall of crumbling ginger brick, but one of the bricks was missing and in the cave lived a tiny man. A lover of tweed and wool and tasseled loafers that shimmied with each step, the man walked to the edge of the cave, a Yorkie clinging on to him like a comma. He was one inch tall and middle-aged with black eyes, Margo saw, that when looking at hers showed a gleam of mischievous recognition. To borrow an expression that she would grow to despise only after using it time and time again when recalling that first spark of illogical affection, Margo felt as though she had known him all her life.

And struck with the need to do something about him, to do anything, she named him Harold.

They'd met by happenstance on another unremarkable afternoon in August when the sun was shining but the rain fell in slashes. Margo's stepmother, Wanda, had hijacked the living room with her bizarre movies and white zinfandel. Always the last to stroll into a room, Wanda had been told that she had a presence. She had tried to become an actress known all over the world, but she never got any farther than the Texas-Louisiana border because life sometimes can be that way. Now she lay on the sofa, naked as a skating rink, belting out her failed monologues:

"I had to sit next to him, praying and drinking alone with him, listening to his dirty jokes. I had to drag him into bed with my bare hands. But after that last indiscretion— I said, That's enough of this! So I won control over this house—control over him and everything. He didn't dare fight back, and look what it's cost me! Nobody in this world can possibly know what winning has cost me."

"Must be terrible," said Harold. He bounced the Yorkie in his arms, looking past Margo. "Parents, you say? What a bunch of manure!"

"Not really," Margo said. She'd actually seen a bunch of manure the time Wanda had had it delivered in a truck that dumped it right onto her father's convertible.

"Why *is* it that parents are so boring?" Harold said. "Because they're groan-ups." He laughed at himself. Margo joined in but too late. The Yorkie, startled by the noise, tried to make eyes with anybody.

Each night Margo listened with her eyes half closed as Harold told her stories. Softly, he read about an ancient wedding, the girl marooned from some desert, the king punch-drunk in love, the castle dually filled with golden light and the mercy of God. "I *am* black, but comely," he read. "Look not on me, because the sun has looked on me. Tell me, O you whom my soul loves, where you feed. Put me like a seal over your heart. Like a seal on your arm. For love is as strong as death."

"Don't read about them," Margo said quickly. "They're dead."

Next door a band was playing. A muffled horn-and-flute arrangement drifted dreamily through the air like jellyfish. Through the library windows Margo saw her father and his wife dancing brain-to-brain.

"They're dead," Margo said again.

Each time she considered this, her mind swirled and crashed. It was through Harold that she first understood that love had had its own life before her, and would after her. For a few minutes she could not forgive him.

Harold closed the book, leaned forward, elbows on his knees. To soften the blow, he told her that she would be his forever, that he would never let her go, that she better not even think about trying to leave. And wanting to hear him make more promises, because the more promises, the better, Margo said that she was determined to run away.

"If you run," said Harold, "I'll find you."

"Then I'll disappear."

"But if you disappear you'll still be you," he said. "And I'll still be the one who finds you." Sighing, Margo ran a hand over coarse bangs that smoothed out but came back in a wave. "Come close," Harold said. He spread his arms to grasp both nostrils and licked the tip of her nose.

Wanda appeared from the bedroom, her hair curled and quaking in irritation. She was carrying a bucket of ammonia that she splashed on Margo's father, Gary, who was reclining on the sofa. Gary scrambled around, all squirming legs and arms, stood up, rushed after her, and shut the door with a precise slam. Margo heard the crash of picture frames and penny jars and a giant bottle of perfume through the bedroom and into the den.

But she was hardly concerned, because she was thinking about Harold. She loved to think about Harold. She loved to remember the way he waddled to the edge of the cave and into her life. She loved that he wore tweed and wool exclusively and that before taking a seat, he pinched the fabric covering his knees. She loved who she became when she was with him—which was almost nothing, small, in its place, acknowledged. She wanted mostly to outlove him.

Margo went into the library and waited. She waited

and waited, and the suspense was delicious before it became painful. Then here came Harold and the Yorkie, who barked once at the sight of her. Harold set down the dog, removed his glasses, and took a long time to find a pocket in which to place them. Margo leaned forward, tempted to help him. He looked at her quickly, surprised and repulsed by her hunger.

Don't be, Margo didn't say. She didn't even want to say *don't*. *Don't* was negative and negative was bad like death was bad. She wanted to live.

And as though reading her mind, Harold said, "It's too bad you can't come live with me. I've got a nice, cozy house. From the den window you can see the most beautiful trees in the world—sunsets that would bring a tear to your eye." As evidence he dragged a finger down his cheek.

"Do you have a library?" Margo heard her voice say.

"Of course," said Harold. "It's made of bricks from some place that doesn't even exist anymore. And I have bookcases filled with books from all over. I have children's books, self-help books, rare books, cookbooks—"

"Are any of the bricks missing?" Margo said, looking past him. "Is there a hole in the wall? Do you see anyone standing in the hole?"

Harold leaned back, looking wary. "I can check," he said. With that he stood and walked into the darkness. Alone, Margo and the Yorkie regarded each other with pity. Then contempt. Harold came back wiping his face with a satin handkerchief. He pinched the fabric above his knees before sitting down. Then he told her when she already seemed to know. "There sure is."

Like a doll inside another doll, by Harold's account there was another brick wall, in which there was another cave, in which there was another tiny man, this time named Ahmed.

Ahmed, she thought fearfully. Whoever he was, she feared she might want to love him, too. She feared she might want to love him more than she wanted to love Harold.

This discovery incited something in Margo. Her head felt small and full of coins. She remembered the desert princess looking for her soul and not finding it. It was terrible not to find things, but it was terrible to find them too.

Margo sent Harold back into the cave and he returned to report that in the next cave was the next man, a Devonté Washington-Myers.

But Margo wanted to know, "Is there anybody else?" And in the next cave was the next man, this time named Ralph.

"Is there someone else?" Margo wanted to know. She filled up with surprise after surprise. Harold started to speak but picked up the Yorkie and turned away. He walked deep into the cave on soundless male footsteps. Every so often he called out, "Yes . . . Yes . . . Yes . . ."

Candy Boii

SAM J. MILLER

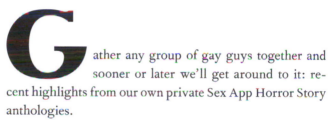

Gather any group of gay guys together and sooner or later we'll get around to it: recent highlights from our own private Sex App Horror Story anthologies.

You would not believe the body odor on this guy—I threw those sheets away, like even if the laundromat got the stink out of the linen they'd never get it out of my mind, *you know?*

In the middle of me blowing him, this guy goes, Wow, is that an actual old-school Nintendo? And then we're done and I just want him to get the fuck out, he turns the thing on and starts playing!

Generally pretty tame, as horror stories go. The real stuff, the true trauma, we keep to ourselves. The guy who didn't stop when we said no—the one who took the condom off halfway through without telling us—the one we kept sucking on even after we saw the sores—all real downers, plus none of us are in a hurry to let our friends see how we are weak, or how we are scared.

Every time, I stay silent. Once in a while I'll toss out something trivial, to throw them off the scent—*Dude started crying, really blubbering, said he promised his wife he wouldn't do this anymore*—because if they ever heard my real story, they'd never believe it. And if they did believe it, it'd ruin their whole day. Possibly also the entire sacred enterprise of app-assisted promiscuity.

This was two years back, now. Saturday: the night when you're most hopeful of finding a fuck for the ages. Ten p.m.: the time when you're most miserable, realizing once again that you won't be getting lucky with a guy uphill from you on the Hotness Slope; you'll have to settle for one of the downhill dudes. Or say fuck it and crawl into your own empty bed.

Springtime. My open window brings in screams, laughter, sirens. I'm toggling between three separate apps—woofing or growling at strangers—responding to innumerable instances of *sup* or *hey* or *u looking* or *want head?* Wondering why that dude I had such a great conversation with last week, when I couldn't have any fun because I had to get up early the next day, is ignoring me entirely tonight.

And there he is, ~700 feet away—thick beard, thick spectacles—looking younger than the 33 he says he is: Candy Boii. Handsome, sure, but nothing superhuman. So I got no problem hitting him up.

Hey, I say. *What are you up to?*

Candy Boii: *Watching horror movies. You?*

ColbyJack (which is me): *Reading. I'm Colby, by the way*

Candy Boii: *I figured. You a big cheese fan?*

ColbyJack: *Who isn't?*

Candy Boii: *No one I want to know*

Here an eyebrow rises, at his failure to respond to my name with his own, but some guys are like that. Skittish about anything that points to their true self. As if the sex-thirsty self is something separate.

ColbyJack: *Looking for anything?*

Candy Boii: *Trying to get this dick sucked*

ColbyJack: *I may be able to help you out with that*

A photo follows. Candy Boii in a mirror, brandishing an admirable erection. Backlit, angled oddly, his face half lens-flare.

My heart hammers, in the silence of my slowed breath. I'm secure and alone on my couch, but my body responds like I'm standing beside a stranger in a bar. Or like a prey animal alone on the winter plains.

We think we're safe, speaking through software. But we're not. We've already let them in.

ColbyJack: *Yum*

Wind tugs a curtain, rough as a pair of hands on a boy's hips. Waiting for a response, trying not to get too excited—plenty of conversations progress to this point only to fizzle out when one's correspondent gets a better offer—I head for the bathroom.

After peeing—an awkward affair, semi-erect—I stop at the window and breathe deeply. The city is so big. So many people are awake in it. So many monsters. So much harm can befall me.

Not that this is specific to the city. It'd been the same back home, looking out to where farmland ran aground against pine forests. All of it just as crowded with monsters.

Waiting for me when I get back to my phone, that happiest of messages: *Album Unlocked*.

First photo: Candy Boii naked and hairy in a darkened hallway somewhere. Mouth slack with what looks like hunger.

Second photo: a human male, extremely dead. Headless; impeccable pecs; three lovely star tattoos; a black cavity wide open below the rib cage. Arms folded in; fingers curled oddly gracefully. Grasping nothingness.

Third photo: Candy Boii standing between two pine trees, pointing at three letters carved into one.

Fourth photo: a selfie of Candy Boii fucking some fit thing—impeccable pecs; extremely alive; three star tattoos on his side.

What the fuck dude, I want to type. *You sick fucking fuck*, I try to say.

Candy Boii: *You like*

My fingers freeze, unable to tap a single letter.

Candy Boii: *Come get some of this*

I know I should call the cops, help stop this evil motherfucker. But fear overwhelms outrage, anger, concern for my fellow man. I block him, I log out, turn off my phone, go to the bathroom to try to throw up.

The pine trees are what fuck me up the worst. That's how I know this is no poseur trying to freak strangers out with gory photos from the Dark Web, or garden-variety human murderer.

The initials carved into the tree were mine. I'd done it myself, when I was fifteen, and I'd never told a soul about it.

I uninstall the app. Spend another half hour on the bathroom floor.

Weeks go by, before I have the strength—or the horniness—to download and open up that app again. No sign of Candy Boii, but I'd blocked him so of course there wouldn't be.

Unless he's using a different name. A different face.
He could be any of these boys.

He's out there still. I know he is. Sometimes, mid-brunch, between hilarious sex app stories, I wonder which of my friends have hit him up. What he showed them. What little cracks it opened up in them.

We focus on the wrong fears. The man who might chain you up and torture you to death, or inject you with something unspeakable, or have a perfectly pleasant time but then come back later to rob and maybe murder you. As long as we stay alive, unharmed—as long as we can walk away—we think: we're fine.

The real danger is how we open ourselves up. What we let in, when we believe ourselves to be safe. We let them in.

Like Klingon Birds-of-Prey, which can't fire when cloaked, we must drop all our defenses before we can engage. Once Candy Boii broke me open with a pine tree photo, I could see how it had been happening all along. How, long before that warm wet May night, even the most banal chats had been planting seeds beneath my skin. So many unsolicited glimpses into the harrowed, salted soil of the human heart. The boy who'd been fucked by fifteen men in six meth-assisted hours, thirsty for one more. The guy whose username was I'm Lonely, which ruined my whole day. I've heard hundreds of terror tales, had countless creepy close calls, and I can say with certainty that there is nothing scarier than a close-up shot of another human being's brokenness.

The Unhaunting

KEVIN NGUYEN

I

After Priscilla died, Carson's only hope was that he'd be haunted. She'd left this world suddenly—a heart attack, as if to spite her perfect health, as if the world were conspiring to make Carson tragically miserable.

Once she was in the ground, Carson waited alone in the bedroom they had shared for three and a half years. He wasn't sure how Priscilla's presence would manifest itself. Perhaps a movement in the dark, maybe a breeze that would rustle the sheets. Or an astral projection? Carson missed his beloved so much that he would've been satisfied with a cold shudder, the feeling that she had passed through him.

The first night, Carson lay awake, anxious, in the hope Priscilla would make an appearance. But each painful minute gave way to morning, and Carson was left feeling disappointed, even a bit angry. No matter. She would materialize on the second night, he thought. That turned out to be wishful thinking, as the days went on, a week passed, and Carson remained unhaunted. Where had Priscilla gone? What was Carson doing wrong? He decided to google it.

It turned out there were a great number of things that Carson could have been doing wrong. A subreddit about interactions with the afterlife, r/haunts, was full of tips and tricks and hacks, none of which were particularly consistent. One user recommended incense, another suggested candles (not lavender), but everyone agreed it helped to burn something. There were varying opinions on the effectiveness of incantations—some felt the words could be powerful forms of summoning, others found it useful just as a means of maintaining focus.

Still, Carson practiced the easiest of rituals. Lights always off, of course. Open windows, Reddit advised, allowed spirits to enter more easily. It was cold out, but Carson was more than happy to bundle up to heighten his odds. A YouTube tutorial also had a handful of ideas, like spreading dirt on the floor to make the room feel "more earthy." Certain patterns for candles (not lavender!) should attract specters with more ease. Still, none of it worked. The internet was a crapshoot, really, but as one YouTube commentator put it, "Ghosts only emerge under specific spectral conditions that depend on them." The problem wasn't Carson, necessarily. It was Priscilla.

II

The feeling of cold, damp fingers; the musty scent of hair; an embrace of wet skin and jagged bone. Weeks went by, and Carson could only conjure these sensations in dreams.

After expressing his woes to a close friend, Carson was referred to a specialist. He would be expensive, the friend warned, but Carson had nothing left to lose. He'd lost everything already.

The initial phone call was strange. Carson felt it fair to ask about the man's accreditations and background—shaman? witch doctor? exorcist?—but the response was a light scolding that those terms were outdated and lightly offensive. He was simply known as Derek, the guy who could get the ghosts. Still, Derek was able to detail his track record. Carson's case was not unusual—just particular. Every ghost was unique, after all.

Carson put down a significant deposit, and a couple hauntless nights later, Derek showed up at his front door. His appearance was different than Carson had expected, more normal. He came armed with a few Tupperware containers. Carson had imagined someone arriving with an otherworldly, mystical aura to them. This guy had the fastidious energy of a housecleaner.

In fact, the first thing Derek did was clean the dirt from the bedroom. What is this, he asked, a nursery? You hoping your dead wife sprouts from the ground? The phrasing forced Carson to hold back tears, and he immediately hated the man. Still, there was an efficiency to how he worked. Derek began rearranging the furniture.

Did Carson have more framed photos of his wife, he asked, which sent Carson to the other rooms of the house to pull pictures off the wall and present them to Derek, who then piled them on the bed in a rather disorderly fashion. Did Carson have more of his wife's clothes, Derek wondered, and so Carson went to the closet and pulled out all of her dresses, shirts, pants, underwear even. Though it felt uncomfortable presenting his wife's undergarments to a complete stranger, Derek appeared confident. All the clothes were dumped on the bed.

The secret, Derek explained, was quantity, volume. If you wanted to be haunted, you needed to bring as many signals into the room as possible. Ghosts, like in Priscilla's case, couldn't find their way. The afterlife was confusing, a labyrinth, lost souls learning how to navigate distant planes in order to return to this one, to ours. Yeah, okay, Carson said, impatiently. Listen, Derek went on, I've never had trouble finding a ghost that wanted to be found.

As night fell, Derek continued scanning the room. He checked the closets, opened drawers, flipped the light switch several times, all for reasons Carson couldn't understand but had to trust were done with the confidence of experience and expertise. Derek had, after all, nearly a five-star rating on Yelp. He laid down a series of blankets, cast dried rose petals on the floor, set out an array of candles (NOT LAVENDER!!!!) of varying heights and widths throughout the room. Then he pulled out a large tome from one of his Tupperware bins—a massive, aged book—and flipped to a bookmarked page. He began chanting a phrase over and over. It wasn't in English, but a language that Carson couldn't make out. Maybe Portuguese. And as Derek repeated the incantation, the room began to shake. A wind blasted in through the windows. The candle flames seemed to grow, illuminating the room. Carson watched as Derek's pupils turned white. Outside, the clouds began to swirl, opening a path for the moonlight to shine directly into the room. It's finally happening, Carson thought. Priscilla, my love, we will be reunited soon.

But in the chaos, nothing emerged. Eventually the wind stopped blowing, the candle flames returned to normal, and the clouds returned to concealing the moon. Derek had run out of breath and could chant no longer.

Wait, don't stop, Carson pleaded. But Derek, whose eyes were back to normal, could only muster a head shake. He'd done everything he could, but Priscilla would not appear. Derek was excellent at his job, but no matter how good he was at summoning specters, it would always be impossible to call on a ghost who did not want to appear.

What did he mean, exactly, that Priscilla did not want to appear?

I dunno, man, Derek said. That seems like something between you and her.

Could it have been possible this whole time that it was no lack of skill or effort on Carson's part, but the fact that Priscilla was not looking for him at all? How could that be true, that his beloved was not searching for him? Priscilla would never abandon him. Not like this. Not after he'd tried so hard to make it work. This was typical Priscilla—selfish, unkind. Carson had never been anything but supportive, even in the worst of times, and now, after death, she couldn't muster the effort to haunt him once. Just once! He asked so little of her and yet—

Derek finished packing his things, but the man was still rambling. With his Tupperware tucked under his arms, it seemed best to Derek just to leave his disappointed client as he was.

He could hear the man going on and on still, even as Derek made his way downstairs, past the hallway full of empty spots where photos used to hang. Even outside, as he packed his belongings in the trunk of his old sedan, the angered sounds of the man could still be heard in the distance. Indignation, it seemed, traveled far.

As the house disappeared in Derek's rearview, he wondered if the man understood what had happened to him. This man was reckoning with the fact that, now, he was truly alone. But the thing he still hadn't comprehended was the lesson of it all: that it was likely his fault.

But whether this guy would understand that was not Derek's concern. He had other clients, easier ones. People with ghosts who didn't feel better off gone.

The Marriage Variations

MONIQUE LABAN

1

When your husband told you he would be sleeping in a separate bedroom, and you complied, you suspected some health problem. After all, you heard those moans at night and wondered if he was gnashing his teeth, curled on the bathroom floor. But every morning, he woke you with the smell of coffee, a couple slices of buttered toast, and a smile, as if you had spent your whole marriage like this. Then you suspected a late-night addiction. You checked his video game controller for warmth when he left for work. Both bedrooms have TVs, and matching armoires, and bay windows overlooking the sea. Everything about the rooms looks the same, in fact, except for his console and controller.

Your husband is obsessive, training to be the top player

of his intramural soccer team; a week of feeding you omelets until they met your family's high standards. Surely he's spent night after night in bed, defeating demons, saving princesses. You wonder if your husband plays as a demon, a princess, or a different creature entirely.

Video games never interested you. He told you about one with angry goddesses and adventures to the underworld, but you forgot the details immediately—you were late to the real estate agent's walk-through inspection. You told him, on the steps of your new seaside cabin, that this was a *real* adventure.

As you lie awake with the moans, the scraping, whatever other noises you refuse to put an image to, you hope he is playing a game, acting out fantasies through the body of a monster.

One night, the noises are unbearable. You aren't to disturb him, but you will break if this continues. If you intend to learn their cause, go to 2. If you must escape these ghastly moans, go to 3.

2

You remember the story your husband told you now, don't you? With your phone flashlight on, it comes to you as you climb down the stairs, slower than your shadow. You know the game he plays, a myth about a woman who learns her lover's divine nature and how he vanishes upon this knowledge. She searches for him anyway, more in love after her discovery.

Perhaps your husband is hiding something shameful. If you force him to reveal himself, if you accept the cause of these moans, will he disappear? Is knowing the truth worth this risk?

You hear a bang. In the light, you see that the cat has knocked the keepsake box off the hallway shelf. Out spill childhood photographs of your sister and two brothers. They never liked your husband.

His door opens on the cat's commotion. He stares at you, blue eyes wide. If you confront him about the noises, go to 4. If you return to bed and seek counsel from your family in the morning, go to 5.

3

The tide rumbles up the shore and the foam licks your toes. If only you could sleep standing up, feet in the sand and the breeze on your neck.

"Hello there," says someone calling from the sea. You search for the voice and spot a beautiful woman in a white dress, floating in the water. You recognize her as one of your husband's ex-wives.

"I thought you were dead," you say.

"I am," the woman says.

"We all are," say the other beautiful women floating along the shore, all your husband's ex-wives.

"We'd have been good friends," the first ex-wife continues. "Our deaths weren't his fault, really. His mother was the true terror."

The other ex-wives agree heartily. They guard you as you sleep. When you return to the cabin, go to 4 to confront your husband. Go to 6 to investigate your mother-in-law.

4

"Have you been all right?"

"Never better. Why do you ask?"

"Then what's been going on every night?"

"What? Every night?"

"Moaning? Thudding? Wails?"

"From you?"

"No, from you."

"Are you having those dreams again?"

"No, that's not what this is."

"Have you been taking your pills? What's going on?"

"I can't sleep. You're loud."

"I don't know what you're talking about."

"Yes, you do. Why won't you tell me?"

"No, something is wrong with you. You need help."

If you wish to believe your husband and end the

conversation, return to 1, having learned nothing. Go to 7 to press on.

5

The slow Wi-Fi distorts your brothers' laughter through the Skype call.

"Remember the keys?" your sister says. Your husband has a ring of keys that he keeps in his inner coat pocket. Your sister once asked what they were for, and he spent the whole evening explaining each one. There was one left whose use he couldn't recall. He went silent when your sister suggested he dispose of it.

"That's just how he is," you say in defense.

"We don't trust him," your brothers say. "He and his family are strange."

"And now you're sleep-deprived?" your sister asks. "What's he hiding?"

"We didn't think you two would last," they all say.

If you need to clear your head, go to 3. If you look into his family, go to 6.

6

You find his late mother's scallop-shell earrings in his night-stand's drawer. He was a mama's boy, but you were scared of her and not without reason. She tested you viciously before the wedding—adhering to her strict weight-loss diet, spending a week's worth of wages to gift her the pricey beauty supplies she wanted.

"You are stunning," she told you. "He has such good taste in wives."

Even after proving yourself to her, you knew she resented you for taking her son. Perhaps the nights are punishment from beyond the grave.

If you are ready to confront your husband, go to 4. If you seek counsel from your family, go to 5.

7

"What's the problem here?"

"Why can't you talk to me?"

"We're talking now."

"Then tell me what's going on."

How has communication between the two of you crumbled so steadily?

"You're the one making a problem out of nothing."

You miss him next to you at night. The bed is too large without him. The blankets don't bring you warmth.

"I really don't know what you're talking about. Stop this nonsense."

Perhaps this is as far as you will get. Return to 4 if you

must continue this game with him. Go to 8 once you realize there is no possibility of winning.

8

Neither of you speaks to the other for the rest of the day.

Hasn't he noticed how your long black hair has gone rough? You forget and repeat tasks so often that you find yourself with four new ChapSticks but can no longer locate your phone. What would it take for him to admit that everything is wrong?

Is anything, indeed, wrong, or is this how things have always been? The direction they would always take? When you sleep that night, or try to, you wonder when you will break, or if you've already broken.

In the morning, there is coffee, toast. If you could have tried harder, go to 2. Go to 3 if you just want peace.

The Family Dinner

MICHELE ZIMMERMAN

The forest—autumn crisp, deep purple. The stone hut—overwarm, cluttered. Inside, identical twin sisters cook meat stew over a stove.

Each sister has a gap between her two front teeth. Each has a permanent blemish between her eyebrows. Each has a scar on her left shoulder—dips in the skin that came naturally at birth. They are separated in age by two and a half minutes. But that's nothing, they are one and the same.

Together they stir the blood and remnants of the girl in the pot over the wood-burning stove.

Each sister has seven piercings on each earlobe. Each has a ring for every finger on her right hand. Each keeps wrists and neck bare.

Their mother is ash in a jar on a shelf above their bed.

Wrapped around their mother is where the opal pendant should hang.

One sister pinches red and brown seasonings from glass vials; the other stirs the pot with a long, splintered spoon. Together they breathe in the rich scent, rear their heads back, and spit.

Each sister has one blackened big toenail. Each has an extra bone in her left heel. Each sister hated her daddy.

His ashes were thrown to the wind some years ago.

When the pot boils, the sisters place heavy stoneware plates and cups upon the table. Garlands of raccoon paws encircle the plates. The candelabras are lit. They serve each other dinner. They pour dark liquid into the other's cup and drink deeply in unison.

Each sister has a bulging disc near her lower spine that pains her in damp weather. Each sister has legs like broomsticks, long and shapeless. Each sister fears loneliness, strangers, and deep water.

From across the table one sister notices a lump underneath the fabric of her sister's shirt. Large, oval, resting in the center of her collarbone. Their ash-mother's pendant.

She points toward this stolen difference.

The sister wearing the pendant stops chewing. She smiles through her mouthful of little-girl stew. She has something her sister does not. She has.

The sister who has not, lunges across the table.

Cups turn over, liquid splashes out. Plates are shoved and food is lost. Candelabras are extinguished, paws are disturbed. She holds a fork to her sister's neck. She pulls the pendant out from under her sister's clothes. She slaps her sister hard cross the face when her sister starts to laugh.

Identical twin sisters pull each other to the floor.

They tumble and twist. They anticipate each other's movements, dodge each other's fists and forks. The sister who has, laughs until she can no longer breathe. The sister who has not, hisses like a cat. She weeps black tears.

At the end of it all, the sister who has stands up. She pulls the sister who has not, up by the arm, and walks her to their bed. She takes the pendant off and wraps the chain of it slowly around the jar of their mother. She smiles at her twin and kisses her on the lips. She dries her sister's tears.

Together they return to the table to finish the remnants of their meal.

Afterlives

BENNETT SIMS

They visited Sicily that weekend. Boeing crashes were in the news, so throughout the flight over the Mediterranean their talk was of turbulence, burial at sea. Driving into Palermo, he paused at a memorial beside the highway, an obelisk monument to the 1992 Capaci bombing, when the Mafia had packed thirteen drums of Semtex and TNT beneath the road and remotely detonated them under a judge's motorcade. Local seismographs, she read aloud from her phone, had registered the explosion as an earthquake. Later, at lunch, talk turned to respect for the dead: soldiers recovering fallen bodies from battlefields; mountaineers carting down frozen climbers' corpses. He cited Antigone's fidelity to Polyneices, sprinkling earth over his cadaver to short-circuit its state-mandated fate as carrion, food for dogs and vultures. Would you do that for *me*? she asked. He thought about it. He had never been sentimental about funerary rituals. It made no difference to the dead, was his feeling. After he died, the career of his corpse—whether it was buried, burned, exposed to scavengers; whether left at sea, or on a mountainside, or on the side of a Sicilian highway—would be a matter of no consequence to him. He certainly wouldn't want her to get herself killed recovering it. But when he considered what he would realistically do in the same situation—for instance if they were stranded in an apocalyptic wasteland, he imagined, and one afternoon she was late coming home, and at sunset he noticed a weird scrum of wild dogs in the distance, and raising his binoculars he saw that what they were all fighting over was her corpse—his eyes surprised him by watering, not in the daydream but in reality, there at the restaurant. He described the dog scenario to her. Yes, he said, if I found a pack of wild dogs devouring your dead body, I think it would enrage me. I would kick them off you and try to bury you. That's the sweetest thing you've ever said to me, she said. But what if—he knew what she was going to ask before she asked it—what if it wasn't wild dogs? What if it were a pack of shar-pei puppies? Shar-peis were his family pet, his favorite breed. He loved to kiss their chubby, wrinkled cheeks. Often, to cheer him up while they were at work, she texted him GIFs of shar-peis. The last had been a looping clip of a shar-pei attempting to eat a strawberry off a hardwood floor: its cheeks were so heavy that they draped like theater curtains over the narrow aperture of its mouth, and each time it reared forward to snap at the strawberry its jowls made contact long before its jaws did, knocking the fruit across the floor like a hockey puck. He pictured a pack of puppies trying to nibble at her like this, as stymied by her remains as by the strawberry. If it were shar-peis, he admitted, I might just say, She's in a better place now. A better *place*?! Yes, he said, and why not a better place? Wouldn't you rather be buried in a puppy than a pyramid? But as soon as he said this he was struck by an eerily vivid mental image of a shar-pei: the dog was staring off in profile, solemn, the image in black and white. The camera of his mind's eye zoomed in on the dog's face, until gradually its gray cheek had filled the frame, then kept zooming in farther, magnifying its wrinkles to abstraction; seen up close, the wrinkles became a network of deep crevasses, with the multicursal lininess of a maze, and as the zooming camera approached this maze he could make out a human figure far below in it, a pale shape stumbling through one of the corridors with arms outstretched, and when finally the camera descended into this trench, bringing the trapped figure into focus, he saw that it was her, lost, distraught, doomed to wander forever through the cheek-flab labyrinth of the Leviathan who had swallowed her. He described what he had seen to her. It's a premonition, she said. Now you know what will happen if you feed me to shar-peis. I'll haunt you so bad. They left the restaurant and spent the weekend in archaeological parks, scrambling over the ruins of ancient temples and theaters, climbing collapsed column drums like boulders. On their last afternoon, driving back to the airport, they paused to admire a work of land art along the highway. A quilt of immense concrete blocks had been cast down a hillside, two acres of white rectangles with a network of narrow pedestrian paths running through them. Known as *The Great Crack*, she read aloud from her phone, the piece had been constructed as a memorial to the 1968 earthquake, which had leveled the town of Gibellina, killing hundreds. The concrete blocks had been cast according to the layout of the city: the gridded paths mapped onto its roads and alleys, while the blocks—which had been infilled with rubble and furniture from the ruins—stood in place of its buildings. Gibellina's real ruins, collapsed houses and churches, were still visible around them, on the outskirts of the sculpture. And just down the highway was Gibellina's real cemetery, with its rows of mausolea, neighborhoods of squat concrete houses for the dead. They were the only people there. They approached the monument together, entering one of its pathways at random. The blocks rose as high as their heads on either side, and the alley stretched before them in an endless white corridor. Following her, running his fingers along the concrete, he felt like an ant crawling across a tombstone: if an ant descended into the inscription, he imagined—if it entered the canyon of a letter, suddenly funneled forward by the high granite walls of the alphabet rising around it—it would never realize that the path it was tracing was a dead name. She announced that she wanted to see the monument from above, so they climbed toward the top of the hill, where there was a lookout platform. But the grade was steep, and as they trudged upward he had to keep stopping for her. Eventually she called to him to go ahead. He hiked to the platform alone, arriving cold with sweat and out of breath. Turning back, he saw the alleys he had just passed through as a labyrinth of craquelure, black lines fissuring a white surface. He scanned the expanse and found her: a small dark figure, wending through a white trench. A chill of recognition passed through him. When she reached the platform, he did not wait for her to catch her breath. Do you remember my premonition? he asked. He described the vision he had had of her ghost, lost in a shar-pei's wrinkles. She nodded cautiously: Yes? He waved one hand over the maze beneath them. Oh my God, she said. We're dead, he said. I'm really here, she said. It really ate me. We're dead, he repeated, and we don't even know it. We'll never leave this place. Together they stepped off the platform and descended into the monument.

The Story and the Seed

AMBER SPARKS

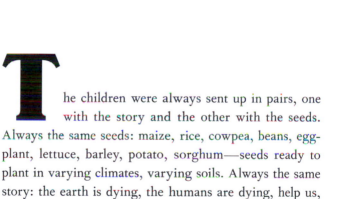

The children were always sent up in pairs, one with the story and the other with the seeds. Always the same seeds: maize, rice, cowpea, beans, eggplant, lettuce, barley, potato, sorghum—seeds ready to plant in varying climates, varying soils. Always the same story: the earth is dying, the humans are dying, help us, house us, accept our gifts.

Hans kept the seeds, and Gzifa kept the story. They were both twelve, both twins, both the only surviving twin. Both lost sisters. Gzifa found Hans suffocatingly kind. His affection transferred easily from his sister, whom he had idolized, to Gzifa. She in turn did not love so quickly. But her father had raised her to be a storyteller, and stories made

Hans easy to manage. As they trained, as they studied, as they traveled to the stars, she spun the story that was theirs alone. It was a comfort to her, too, among the wires and the dials and the antiseptic surfaces of the spaceship. It was a comfort to have a story.

Will the new planet be scary? Hans asked, as they watched the shadows of something unknown move over the viewscreens. The shadows seemed to merge, to bend and bleed into the lush vegetation. Everything was too green, and shimmered in the dim light of this planet's suns. He thought he saw teeth. He rubbed his eyes.

Yes, it will be scary, said Gzifa. It will be covered in forests, and strange new animals will wait in dark corners to devour us.

Hans blanched.

But, said Gzifa, we will find our way. To a place where we can make our new world. She lifted her braids, tucked them into her space suit. She pulled her helmet over her head. That's the story, Hans.

Okay, said Hans. He reached for her hand. And they opened the hatch, their silver-clad bodies pressed together as they stepped through.

This new world moved like a cat: slow, languid, mysterious. There was rain from time to time. Gzifa took out an acid detector, but the rain seemed clean and pure. They moved slowly, too, quiet as they could in their big heavy boots and helmets. It felt humid and hot here. There was a strange sense of waiting; the planet seemed alive to their footfall.

I think they know we're coming, said Hans.

Yes, said Gzifa. That's part of the story, too.

They walked a little way through foliage so dense they couldn't get a good look at the planet's suns. The light seemed to be waning. In this part of the story, said Gzifa, the children stumble upon a secret. She pointed to a bone, then another—Human? Animal? No way to tell—strewn along so regularly it might be a path. A bone path.

Why should there be bones? asked Hans. They had seen no life at all, other than the trees.

It's the evil witch, said Gzifa. She eats children, and throws out the bones. But we're too smart for her.

Why, said Hans, what happens next?

We drop our bread crumbs, said Gzifa. She didn't want to admit that under her helmet, her sweat was cold. Hans reached into his belt, powered up a little gray sensor, and let it fall. As they walked farther from the ship, he dropped another, then another. They walked away from the bones, or tried to—but the macabre little path seemed always to be just ahead. Frustrated, Gzifa consulted an instrument on her wrist. I know we're not walking in a circle, she said. At least, I don't think we are. Behind them, something hissed in the trees.

It will take a long time for the seeds to grow, said Hans.

We have food on the ship, said Gzifa.

I'm hungry, said Hans. He was a muscular boy, and in the way of all twelve-year-olds, he was always hungry.

You know the story, she told him. The children live on

the ship until they build a home. It's long years to make a home, Hans. She thought about her father, his strong brown hands cradling the tiny sprouts, the little green shoots longing for the sun. I'm not the story anymore, her father had told her. Everything in space is starting anew.

They walked for a while in silence, Hans dropping sensors, bones dotting the unchanging landscape. Gzifa thought she saw a skull, but when she blinked, it resolved into smooth strange rocks, alien as any life-form here in this wild place. They heard hissing, almost like cicadas; it grew stronger, until the children came upon a sight so strange that they froze.

A house. A cottage, really, built of brick and wood, ordinary and terrifying. Gzifa had never seen such a house, or lived in such a house; she and her father had traveled the world, nomadic, living mainly in settlements or on bases. Hans, though, was raised in the countryside, and knew these little houses. This one looked like a storybook home: sturdy squat brick with two painted white shutters, a red door, and a crooked little chimney with a plume of smoke that blew sideways in the light breeze. It smelled like something delicious, sweet and salty at once. Both children shuddered at the wrongness of the place.

Do the children go inside the house? Hans asked. In the story? He blinked at her, and she could see his pupils, narrow and scared.

No, she told him. They turn right back around, and they follow the bread crumbs until they reach their ship.

The light was growing dim, was almost gone above the thick tangle of branches and leaves overhead. The hissing was so loud, Gzifa had to turn up her intercom to be heard. She flipped open her sensor app and stared. Nothing. No beeping. No bright blue signals. She stared at the ground. Where was the path home?

Hans, she whispered. Did you power them up?

I did, yes, he said, his skin milk-pale.

Gzifa went to pick up the nearest sensor, just a few feet away. She reached her gloved hand out and, impossibly, the ground came up to meet it. There was a sucking sound. Hans, she said, standing perfectly still.

What?

It's gone. The ground. It—it *ate* the sensor. Just—just swallowed it. Gzifa blinked. She couldn't believe it. This planet was alive, somehow. There was nothing in the story about this.

Hans wasn't listening; he had begun walking, slowly, toward the house. Hans, she shouted, there is no house in the story! It can't be real, she shouted, stop, Hans, but he was moving faster toward that red front door, and it seemed to be grinning, seemed to be tooth-filled, seemed to be dripping, not with paint but blood or something like it, opening, opening. The trees were leaning, branches snapping as they made a tunnel over the boy. *Hans*, screamed Gzifa, but he was already gone, he was inside, and she was watching the door snap shut, Hans's body snap too, limp and red and silver and white.

She ran. The hissing was so loud overhead that it hurt Gzifa's ears. She was shouting, breathless, shouting the story. In this story, she shouted, in this story the children find the bread crumbs easily. In this story, it never gets dark at all. In this story, the children get sent to bed early, get up in the bright sun of morning. In this story—she crashed into the thick trunk of a rubbery tree. She heard a low rumbling sound. She ran on, into the dark, into the hissing, until she suddenly saw it: the blue glow of the sensors.

Blue after blue, she matched her steps to each, heard the pulsing beeps on her tracker. Her tears stopped. Her breathing slowed. The story was still there, underneath. And the children, she whispered, found the bread crumbs. Boot down, boot down, she made her way back to the ship. They saw their home, she said. Gzifa saw the hatch opening, saw the lights of the console. Her father's laugh burst from her. She would find the seeds in the spaceship and she would plant them. She was a person who meant to survive. I'm sending you, her father told her, because you did what your sister and I could not. You lived.

She climbed up the ladder, didn't notice the slight waver, the glow around the spaceship's surface that came from nowhere at all. She pulled herself up and into the ship's interior—into absolute darkness. The trees leaned. The ship's maw widened. She screamed. This isn't the story! The trees wound around her, green over silver. They squeezed.

The earth already told us the story of humans, they hissed.

After a time, the trees returned their gaze to the deep pool of sky. They drank it in, satisfied, noting the winking light of Earth far off, across the wide bowl of space beyond.

3

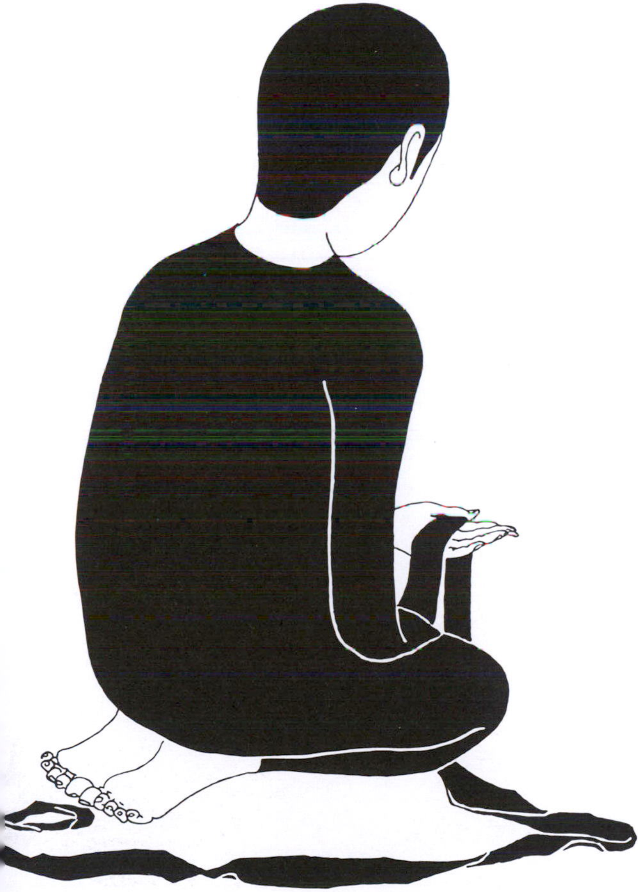

Fingers

RACHEL HENG

The villagers lived in attap houses perched on high wooden stilts, the land by the sea being soft and shifting as it was. That, at least, was the official reason for the stilts.

Yet the children often suffered the unpleasant sensation of having one leg sink knee-deep into the squelching, bubbling mud. As they were pulling their legs out, they'd feel it: gentle fingers wrapping around their plump, sun-browned calves. They'd shriek and jerk their legs up more quickly, and the fingers would slip away.

Parents dismissed these rumors, citing seagrass, mud-skippers, and trapped pockets of air as possible culprits for what the children insisted were fingers. But the children saw how their parents scrutinized the earth as they went about their daily chores. They noticed new designated areas marked with orange tape tied to little metal sticks driven into the ground. Once an area was designated, it was off-limits.

Soon the orange tape was everywhere. It resembled a twisting, winding maze. One might be obliged to take a circuitous route across the entire village just to get to their neighbor's house. It got to the point where everyone added an extra half hour to any journey they had to take. Still, the parents would not admit that the situation was dire. They went about their daily activities with new vigor, often jogging from one place to another in order to make up for the lost time caused by the orange tape.

The children decided that something had to be done. If their parents would not face the fearsome truth lurking beneath their very feet, then they would.

On the appointed night, at the appointed hour, they stole out of their houses. Little shadows came from everywhere in the village, weaving through bushes and trees and orange tape, all heading to the oldest, deepest mud spot in town, one of the first ever designated areas. In their arms, the children carried bedsheets, ragged towels, strips of gunnysacks, old tattered samfu bottoms. They worked quickly, twisting each item into a rope and tying them together. The moonlight that shone down on them gave a pallor to their hands, and their fingers appeared a ghostly white as they knotted and pulled, knotted and pulled.

They looped the rope around the waist of the strongest boy in the village, and then the waist of the next strongest boy, and the next, and the next, until all the children were strung together, and then they tied the end of the rope to one of the sturdy stilts of a nearby house. The idea being that the first boy would lower himself into the mud, allow the fingers to wrap themselves around his calves, but then, instead of jerking away, let them take hold of him. Once the creature had its grip, the boy would plunge his hands into the mud, and grab the fingers around his legs. With their collective strength, they would pull the creature out of hiding. Several of the children from fishing families had snuck nets from their fathers' boats and would have these at the ready for when the monster emerged. It would then be up to the children of the butchers and fishmongers. In their hands glinted their parents' sharpest knives, stolen from busy kitchens and market stalls earlier that day.

The children checked the ropes, the nets, the knives. Everything was ready. They watched as the strongest boy stepped one foot over the orange tape, then the other. Nothing happened at first, and they thought perhaps that patch had dried over, become regular solid ground. But then he began to sink, the mud sending up soft burps around him. He held his arms out high above his head as he sank, as if getting into position for his mother to undress him before bed.

When he had sunk thigh-deep, his face changed, and the children knew that the fingers were creeping across his skin. The boy grimaced and his eyes widened, but being brave as he was, he stayed put, sinking deeper and deeper into the mud. The children waited for the signal. When the mud was up to his hips, the boy plunged his arms into the ground as planned, grabbing the creature that had its grip on him.

"Pull!" he shouted, and the children pulled.

The boy began to emerge from the mud, but as his body inched out of the earth, birds rose from the bushes and the trees around them began to sway. A strange rushing noise filled the air, a noise that sounded like the night itself was whispering a warning. And yet the children kept pulling, their hearts full of bravery and the best of intentions.

"Pull!" he shouted again.

Now the ground began to shake, and the moon itself, so bright, so perfectly round, began to tremble in the sky. The children kept pulling. The boy's knees could now be seen.

"Pull!"

It was then that the trees began to sink into the ground, their ancient, twisting trunks slipping lower and lower into the earth. Yet still the children pulled.

Finally the boy's hands were visible, as were his calves, and around them were the fingers of the creature. Except what they had thought were fingers were in fact thick vines with tendrils protruding from their length, all firmly wrapped around the boy's feet and hands. Roots, the boy realized. The children stared in wonder, little hands growing slack on the rope.

Then the trees began to pull back.

Again the ground and sky shook, again the air was filled with a strange whispering. But this time it wasn't the trees that were sinking, it was the children. First the boy in the mud patch disappeared, his glossy black hair vanishing beneath the mud like an exotic plant subsumed into the soil. Then the next-strongest boy, tied to him on the rope, was drawn kicking and screaming into the earth. Then the next child, and the next. They tried to pull back but it was no use; the trees were stronger than them, of course they were.

Child after child disappeared into the ground, their wet, gurgling cries awakening the parents and drawing them out of their houses. When they saw what was happening, the parents tried to grab on to the children, but were also drawn inexorably into the earth. The trees kept pulling still; the rope of bedsheets and towels proved fatal.

Eventually the last child was sucked into the ground, and along with her, the last parent. Now the night was quiet. Only the wind in the trees and the dull crash of waves was to be heard. Until the stilts of the house to which the children had tied themselves began to creak, a high, keening noise like the cry of an injured bird. The creak ended in a snap that brought the house to its knees, pulling it, too, into the earth.

The trees didn't stop until all the houses were gone, all the fences, all the wheelbarrows, all the clothes carefully strung out to dry earlier that day. When it was over, nothing remained to suggest that a village had ever been there at all, except for one mossy corner beneath an old tree, where, protruding from the earth, was a piece of muddy orange tape.

Carbon Footprint

SHELLY ORIA

Sometimes you gotta risk your life to survive, Jack says and shrugs. He means we need to keep taking the subway: hope for the best, take precautions. We're no car owners, and with the market skyrocketing like it has, that's not changing anytime soon. We can't afford cabs, either, which have gotten much pricier these last few weeks. He's not wrong, my husband. I touch the bone at the top of his shoulder, then slide my fingers halfway to his neck. It's a beautiful manbone, one that exudes power. It's got a name, that bone. I stayed in school long enough to know what I don't know.

My husband flexes his muscles at the touch of my hand. It's what men do: you touch their shoulder bone, they show you strength. There's plenty of ways to manipulate the man you love, and most of them you learn by watching. Overall you could say watching is the sort of thing I've done too much of in my life. I started early, too. First time I saw a man's chest harden at judgment I don't think I was twelve, even. And then I saw that same man's chest buckle at the soft sound of a compliment, and I learned that all can happen in the span of a moment if the woman's a good twister of words, a good singer of their music. *Jacks*, I say, *baby*. I sigh, a whisper of air. *I'm not brave like you.*

My husband feels guilty when I say these words; I can see the color of blame in his eyes. He wishes his schedule allowed him to walk me to the subway whenever I left our apartment. And in his wishing he imagines me a more powerful woman than I am. *Your spine is made of little eyes and ears, baby*, he tells me. *Whenever I open the fridge for a beer, you yell from the bedroom. "Easy on the fizz, Jacks." A Pusher try to make a move on you on the platform? Next thing, we're at his funeral, offering condolences to his mama.*

I say this to Betty Boop the next day on the phone, I say maybe Jack's right, maybe I've been more scared than I need to be. I say, *It's true that I got better instincts than most.* Betty says it ain't right.

Betty and I have been friends since the first nursing home we both worked at, and the thing about spending your days with old people is you get in the habit of saying exactly what you think. *As your man he should make sure you buddy up when he's not around*, she says. Buddying up is what's considered safe now, ever since Pushers started popping up, shoving or kicking people in front of trains. They believe they're saving the planet, according to most rumors, but I don't see how that can be right. *I buddy up with you*, I tell Betty Boop. *When you do it's no thanks to him*, she says. She exhales with agitation. *Maybe he mean well*, she says, *but telling you a Pusher's got nothing on you can get in your head, make you less alert. People die that way all the time*, she says. About a hundred people a day, to be exact: across boroughs and stations, men, women, and children. *Don't worry about me*, I say.

Betty Boop is what Jack calls Betty, and I guess it got in my head. Sometimes I almost slip and call her that to her face. *She'd slap you if she heard*, I say to Jack. *What?* he says. *It's a compliment.*

The next day after our shift, Betty and I walk down the subway stairs and hit a storm of people. Betty looks at me. *This ain't right*, she says. She wants us to U-turn. *What, and walk?* I say. I want to get home in time to cook dinner for Jack. He's been having a hard time: work stress, subway stress. Last night he woke me up shaking. *I dreamt you died*, he said, *I dreamt they pushed you*. *Oh, baby*, I said. I rocked him like a child until we both fell back asleep. *Fine*, Betty says, *fine*. She shakes her head at me. She keeps looking around, keeps looking everywhere. I do the same to show her we got this. The thing about a crowded platform, you're not guaranteed to stay far enough from the tracks to be safe. A wave of bodies rises and falls; I reach for Betty's hand and clench air. I yell her name and the sound is swallowed in the echo. Squeals pierce the air as bones meet gravel. Wheels roll over, then screech to a halt as they do, as they always do, as if in surprise. Trains will be out of commission now for a few hours, until the bodies are removed. I tell myself it's fine. This has happened before—we've lost each other in the crowd. I imagine that I see Jack in the distance; my mind plays this trick on me sometimes when I need comfort. As I climb back up the stairs, my body knows something bad just happened. I call Betty again and again when I get home, text her a million question marks. My breath aligns itself to the web page: inhale on every refresh, exhale on every new list of names that doesn't include Betty's. And then her name is there, staring at me, daring me to stare back. I look away. I turn my back on that screen and go curl up into myself in bed, where I stay for days.

Jack makes pots and pots of tea, leaves full trays on the nightstand even though the food goes to the trash every morning. I keep the blinds shut to keep the darkness in. Jack knows to let me grieve. But on the third or maybe fourth or maybe fifth day, he enters the room with intention. *You gotta eat*, he says. I want to ignore him and go back to sleep, but his shoulders are big and I know he has something important to say. *I'm not hungry*, I tell him. *See, the thing is, baby*, he says, *a body gets weak without food, and we need you strong for Friday*. In the dark of the room I can barely make out his face but I squint at him like we're in the sun. *What's Friday?* I ask. *Your initiation*, he says. I've heard rumors about Pushers' initiation ceremonies but that can't be what Jack is talking about. I sit up and reach for the light switch, but Jack's hand is faster. *There's nothing to see right now*, he says. He leans over and puts his other hand over my heart. *Listen to what you already know*, he says. He's standing over me in an awkward position that would be funny any other time. And maybe it's the shock, or maybe I don't believe Jack's saying what I think he's saying, but whatever the reason: what I do is tickle his armpit. Jack collapses on the bed in surprise. He looks at me. *Is that a yes?* he whispers. *You'll join the underground?* I see terror in his eyes, or maybe the terror is inside me. *Why do I feel like I don't have a choice?* I whisper back. I want Jack to say, Don't be crazy, baby. What he says instead is, *None of us have a choice; our home is on fire*. I know he means the planet but I've never heard Jack worry about the state of the Earth; we don't even recycle. *And pushing people is going to . . . kill the fire?* I ask. *They have data, baby*, he says, *real data, not the bullshit in the news. We're on the express line to nonviability, and mass death is the only means of disruption*. If anyone asked me yesterday, I would have bet my life on Jack not knowing what any of these words meant. Guess if I did that, I'd be dead now.

It is almost dawn when I wake up. Jack is sitting on his side of the bed staring at me. I don't remember how we fell asleep. I don't remember anything at first, but then I do, and the memory hits like the kick of a foot to a soft part. *Who are you?* I ask. *Don't be crazy*, Jack says. *What happens to me if I say no?* I ask. *You won't*, Jack says. *Were you there that day*, I ask, *when Betty . . . ?* Jack closes his eyes. *I want you to know something*, he says. *The feeling you get from pushing a body? You haven't been alive until you've known that rush.* The inside of my mouth is turning to cement. Jack offers his hand to me. *Let me show you*, he says. *Let me take you to the tracks.*

We Came Here for Fun

ALANA MOHAMED

When we found the body it was late. We had gone to Terry's place after Darren messed with some cops. "Just to check in," we all said. She hadn't been around in a minute. But really, we just needed somewhere to drink.

Darren smashed a window and we all climbed in, young drunken limbs tangled together. We moved like a five-headed beast in heat. We were giddy at our own genius: outrunning the cops, some light b&e. We were a force everything else had to react to.

So that's why, when we found the body, no one wanted to see it. School was out. It was time to work full days flipping burgers and let the oil seep out of us at night along with beer and piss and whatever else was haunting our bodies. That's why no one paid attention to Johnny when he screamed.

"Johnny, you're seeing things," we told him. We stepped over the body to get to the couch across her tiny living room. He hiccupped in protest. Terry had always loved him best. We hadn't seen her in days. She looked awful, bloated and pale with a bluish tint to her. It didn't matter. We were there to have a good time and we were going to have a good time.

I settled on the floor with Darren, his body hot with anticipation. Our backs rested against the couch, angled at such a degree that, if we tried, we didn't have to see Terry at all. We lit candles to savor the dark. Johnny stood just short of the body, looking down as if she were a test he hadn't studied for.

Sometimes it made sense not to see Terry for a while. She had dropped out of school and gotten a real job. She was assistant manager at the diner where she fed us doughnuts and refused us beer. I hated her preference for glazed bullshit.

"Wonder where Terry got off to," Jane said to no one.

"Terry's dead, she's right there," Johnny insisted, his voice cracking. Terry had given Johnny a job when no one else would. He was a fan of the doughnuts.

"Johnny, baby, we're just here to have a good time," we tried to explain to him. We weren't here to find a dead body.

We urged him to have a lie down on the couch instead, but he backed up even closer to the window, as if he'd be able to slither back out and rewind time.

Terry once told me I had potential. She meant it kindly, but everyone has potential at sixteen.

I used mine to steal beer from work. That night we were drinking the one that turns blue in the cold. Terry's lips looked more ready to drink.

"It smells in here," Johnny said. "How can you not smell that?"

"That's just the smell of the city," Jane argued. We listed the possibilities. The garbage slush wafting through the broken window, the hint of a gas leak no one could ever afford to fix. Old laundry, moldy bread.

"The smell is coming from right here," Johnny yelled, pointing.

"I think you're having a bad trip, man," Raf said, sprawled out in Jane's arms. We nodded solemnly.

Johnny started to cry, like an idiot. "Why can't you guys see it?"

"See what?"

"The body! Her body." Johnny sputtered. His hand waved over her without making contact.

"Sorry, whose body?"

"Terry's!" It was hard to hear him through the sobs.

"Johnny, what are you talking about?" Darren said with alien sweetness. "Terry's in Miami."

"Miami?"

155

"Yeah, she said we could use her place, remember?" Raf and Jane were holding back giggles, their catching breath a dare. I kept waiting for Johnny to hear it, grab Terry's mottled face, and call our bluff.

But Johnny just stared at the hole we had made in the window. "Why did we have to break in, then?" The uncertainty in his voice filled me with disgust, with glee. The world kept bending to accommodate us.

"More fun that way." Darren shrugged.

Johnny had stopped hyperventilating, but still wouldn't step over the body. "I'm not having fun," he said.

"That's 'cause you're standing there like an idiot," Darren said. "Have a drink." He left my side and in two steps he stood on her chest—its chest. Something cracked. He held a beer out to Johnny, and I shivered.

Johnny hesitated a second too long. Darren made a sound of practiced ambivalence that I recognized from being the bearer of his bad news. When the world denied him his whims, he would blow air from between his lips, shrug, and walk away. He did it then, letting go of the bottle and leaping off Terry's sinking chest. It rolled my way.

Terry never liked Darren much. She claimed he lacked moral fortitude. I always thought he was just bored.

"We should do something," he announced, then added, "to take Johnny's mind off things."

"Yeah! Let's raid her room," Jane said. Everyone ambled over to Terry's closet, like it would hold anything more than her beige, couponed work uniforms.

I reached for the beer, the body in my eye line. She was wearing an oversized shirt, no knickers.

The last time I saw her, she was on duty in those dumb beige pants. I hadn't wanted to see her, but we needed the money since one of Darren's moneymaking ventures had gone to shit. She had sat me down in a roomy booth. We split a doughnut while I feigned interest in scheduling and sick employees. "Oh, everything's fine," I had cut in when she took a breath. "Everything's fine, except I need an abortion and, you know, the clock's been ticking down for a few days, weeks, whatever."

She had gasped and looked sorry for me. She said she'd give me the money, of course, but that I needed to be careful. That I had so much potential. My eyes glazed over and wouldn't unstick until she pulled out her wallet.

My potential was still intact, baby or no. But I knew she thought I was stupid enough to let one happen to me, which was the worst part of the scam. All Darren knew was that she walked around with cash. When she pressed the bills into my hands, I only smarted a little.

I was happy she was dead, I realized. I had been staring at her big, blue body with no particular care, and Johnny had seen. Embarrassed for myself, I looked away.

"You see her too, right?" Johnny asked.

I inched closer to him, to her. He was looking down at me with wild, excited eyes, like Darren sometimes got. I took a deep breath, letting her decay filter through my insides.

"Johnny," I said slowly, slipping my hand inside his, pulling him down. "There's nothing here. Where's the body? Pick it up and show me, if there's a body." The need in my voice was unflattering, ugly. He recoiled at the sound.

But I, I could not help it. I leaned in to taste the body— just a lick of the neck. She went sweet on my tongue. Johnny laughed hard and endless, finally having a good time.

The Barrow Wight

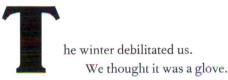

The winter debilitated us.
          We thought it was a glove.
    The winter became subcutaneous.

Blizzards buried parking meters. Plows built roadside balustrades. Schools closed. We exhausted the energizing joy of dramatic snowstorms by January. Were drinking more by February. Catching up on classic movies.

You expect a glove in a melting snow mound. Three days later we realized it was a hand.

Authorities were called. Hospitals contacted. Missing-person reports cross-referenced. We reached out to people we hadn't heard from recently. The authorities were, we assumed, scientific and thorough.

For a week, we saw hands instead of gloves.

Feet instead of boots.

We saw another hand.

The media invaded. We gave the ill-informed, poorly phrased, emotionally contradictory interviews expected from "the people on the street." Got pretty good at them, eventually. Inside jokes and everything.

Another receding snow mound revealed a foot.

After the second hand, we constantly imagined feet. Idle moments at work. When yawns closed our eyes. Blinking away the colored shapes of too-long-stared-at screens. We thought we were prepared.

Maybe we would have been if someone else had found it, not the kind fifth grader who still believed the world is so people can be happy in it. What do they think about a fucking foot in a snow mound? We weren't prepared.

Then a four-day problem with an idiom.

Then . . . (fuck it) the other foot dropped.

The media returned but their tone changed. Mocking derision replaced morbid curiosity, as if behind every question lurked a rhetorical "Can you believe these people? Limbs in their snow mounds? Who's driving their plows, am I right?"

We shared a nightmare of being chased through a dark tunnel. The tunnel narrowed until we crawled. It terminated. An evil approached. We pushed with all our might against the terminus. We broke through, flopping onto slushy ground to a chorus of screams. Bottles dropped. The shattered glass assembled into a surface that reflected a severed hand with a face in its palm.

The use of "applause" radically increased.

Our alcohol drinkers felt their desire for it diminish in direct proportion to the increase in their need for it.

Parents couldn't tell their children to play outside.

Horror movies were absented from sleepovers.

We packed high school basketball games like never before and cheered with unprecedented passion. The team went two and six.

We watched even more TV.

Next was a forearm.

A dog found it. A good dog.

The forearm was put in the morgue with the other limbs. Picture the visage of a freaked-out coroner.

Spring increased the pace of revelation. The rest of an arm up to the shoulder was found the next day, and its partner that afternoon.

A few people left. In public, we politely questioned their commitment. In private, we hated them as we hate elderly relatives lingering in nursing homes.

The high school drama club met after school; at least, we think it was the drama club, because none of the other groups of students would have this conversation; or maybe they would: teenagers are weird. It wasn't even a conversation, just one kid talking. You know, how you just kinda talk yourself into the outside. What are we doing? We're not afraid of this getting out, are we? That'd be stupid. Nobody got in a fight. Nobody drew a gun and accidentally shot someone else. Nobody had sex in the bathroom. Nobody even did drugs. Somebody said they were looking up stuff on the internet because they were bored and Dad was watching college basketball and you do not change the channel when Dad is watching college basketball, so they learned that many scholars theorize that the idea of "barrow wights" originated with Mongolian herdsmen who believed powerful spirits guarded improperly buried bodies and tormented travelers, and the belief in these malicious spirits accompanied them as they swept into Europe, where the spirits were associated with trolls guarding cemeteries in Poland and Hungary, making their way into one unattributed German fairy tale in which the cruelty of a tyrannical prince congealed into a gremlin that haunted his grave, a version of which was adapted into an Arthurian legend—originally composed in France, of course—in which a "burial wraith" tried to trick Sir Lucan the Butler into replacing the dead lord in a tomb, and once in France there was only a channel between these monsters and England, which actually had burial mounds or barrows, *barrow* coming from the Old German for "mountain," and in England they developed a mischievousness that included using dead bodies and the parts thereof in pranks, which many scholars believe was an explanation for the occasional absences of bodies from graves, and it was from these folktales that Tolkein created the "Barrow-wights," now so prevalent in fantasy and horror culture.

Somehow the term *barrow wight* manifested in everyone's minds. If we lost focus, it ended up in open documents and emails.

Thighs and shins of two legs were found at the cardinal directions.

The genitals centered the leg compass.

The torso had to be next. We could do an autopsy. We were thrilled. Autopsy is the highest expression of modern humanity. Another thing we learned.

We held a dark carnival. We dressed as demons to frighten demons. Warty prosthetic noses. Gnarled horns. Hooves over hands. Grizzled branches on our backs. Gleeful in our horribleness. We made curseful noises to banish the curses. Rucksacks of glass hurled against stop signs. Plastic bags fed through snowblowers. TVs dropped from heights. Vicious comfort in our cacophony. We pantomimed cruelty to defuse cruelty. Staged executions. Harmless lashings. Unspecified but unsettling devices. We replaced thrill with fake thrill. Whatever else we felt in consideration of this image of ourselves we defined as coincidental.

The torso was in the sewers.

In a glass case.

Perfectly preserved.

We opened the case.

The torso turned to mulch.

The guy who worked in the garden center, nice enough really, but talked about fantasy sports way too much, said it was organic cedar. But really, could he tell just by looking? It was just a fucking torso. It's fine. He wanted to contribute. We all want to contribute. Most of us don't know how. So we have kids. Hi, kids. We love you.

JOSH COOK

The head should appear soon and end this.

We discussed war heroes.

Uncles who died overseas.

One barrow remained.

The sense of carnival returned. Just the sense.

We vigiled in shifts, with snacks and flasks. Just like ice fishing.

We finally started talking about the Mound Man. We would look in his eyes. We would put him on the internet. We would solve a mystery. This ordeal would rebind what components of our community had drifted apart through capitalism's tectonics.

We would contact the media.

We would give interviews.

Again.

We would sell the movie rights and build a homeless shelter. Or a playground. Or a free clinic. Mound Man Day would be the official start of our spring, a celebration of our triumph.

We would triumph.

The barrow melted.

There was another hand.

Katy Bars the Door

RICHIE NARVAEZ

Less than three hours after she tied the knot, after the escape from a Dutch oven of a church and then the bladder-jarring limo ride to Flushing Meadows Park, after posing for pictures covered in a steady drizzle and the clinging smell of defeated deodorant, and after another long zigzag ride to Izzy's wedding hall, with a quick stop off at a Sizzler, all the patrons staring at her as she taffeta-ed down a cheap wood-paneled hall to a bathroom of greasy yellow tiles, and after arriving and after the first dance to the wrong song ("I wanted 'My Blue Heaven,' *not* 'Tears in Heaven'"), and seconds before the cake was cut, the newly minted Katy de la Cruz (née Guerrera) experienced what she considered an epiphany.

The thunderbolt of insight revealed to her that her

handsome-but-between-jobs new husband, Jesus, thought of her as a prize. Actually, it wasn't so much an epiphany as her overhearing something that her sister said she had overheard: Jesus turning to his best man and saying, "She's a career girl. I ain't gotta lift a finger for the rest of my life."

Later, as Jesus stood next to her, Katy stared into the photographer's flash, just as someone handed her a knife.

She turned to look at Jesus, his bearded cheeks ruddy and glistening, as they both grasped the knife, and she knew that she despised him. Dutifully, she shoved the buttercream-laden cake slice into his face.

They went on to have twins.

Seven years later, her career in market-research analysis well on its way, she let her lover kiss her, his stubble like a cheese grater on her neck. He called himself Roberto, but she called him Romeo in texts to Adriana, her best friend and alibi. He was fit, dabbled in sales, and was very talented with his lips—except that he used them too much to talk about an upcoming zombie apocalypse.

For that reason, she broke up with him. But also because when he looked at her with emo eyes behind big black glasses, she felt that he, too, saw her as a prize.

Afterward, she sighed for a year.

But then the zombie apocalypse actually did arrive, and Katy felt pretty chagrined.

Adriana was the one of the first people she called. Before Katy could say anything, Adriana said, "Oh my

god! Do you think a claw hammer is enough to kill these—
is *undead* the correct term? *Zombies* just seems culturally
appropriated."

"I only know what I see on cable," Katy said. "Do you
have a shotgun or something like that?"

"C'mon, Katy, we're not those kind of people."

"Listen, the kids are with their grandparents in Florida.
No one's answering the phone, and Jesus's t—"

The line went kaput. As did the Wi-Fi. And thus the
world.

In the master bedroom behind Katy, shirtless and in
sweatpants, her husband grunted about brains. She barred
the door with the giant TV console and one of the kids'
larger Lego sets. Jesus banged at the door with more *oomph*
than he had ever shown for anything in life.

Meanwhile, outside the window, emerging from underneath the blooming dogwood tree across the street, taking his time as always, came Romeo. How inappropriate of
him to come to her house while her husband was home. But
Romeo was a zombie now, too, his lovely lips reduced to
monosyllabic muttering.

She barred the front entrance with a credenza and a coat
rack, both from Raymour & Flanigan. Sitting on it and sip-
ping cabernet, Katy searched for another epiphany.

To both these zombies—*better?: people who are no longer
living*—she had been a prize. For her sex, her steadiness, her
salary. Now she was a prize again, but for her brains. And
not in a complimentary way. But what was the prize she was

seeking, the thing she could win for herself, to make her life worthwhile?

What was it she looked for in Romeo? Was he, as her therapist suggested, just a prize as well for her? When she'd broken up with him, he sent a dozen poems he had written himself, several drafts of a suicide note, and fifty-four nude selfies. She deleted all but one.

When Jesus had found out about Romeo, he said, "This shit has to stop," but then confessed to a ten-year "emotional affair" with someone he met online gaming. Katy slept in the guest room after that, which was fine since Jesus was a blanket hog. In the dark, she had wondered what it was she had loved in him. Was it how he wouldn't break a sweat as he worked his way through a plate of buffalo wings? Or was he—as Adriana had suggested—just a replacement for Papi?

Oh, Papi. Papi had never talked about prizes. He had never said much of anything, and when he did, it was about the weather—things like "It's gonna be cold today" or "It's gonna be hot today." Every once in a while, though, after a few Drambuies, he would pat her head and say things like, "Katy, *mi niña*, life is all sacrifice."

He was right. Because now she had to sacrifice herself. There was no cellar to hide in, no helicopter waiting on the roof. Letting her husband be the one to consume her seemed like the proper, wifely thing to do. But surely Romeo would do it with more imagination.

But then she had another epiphany. She didn't have to go one way or the other. She had a third choice.

If she remembered right, Jesus had the keys to the car in his sweatpants pocket, the car that was parked in the driveway, the driveway across which Romeo was currently, fitfully shuffling.

Fine, then. She would move the furniture. In a minute. But first she poured herself more cabernet, and then she made a double-headed pike out of a stainless-steel curtain rod from Crate & Barrel, and once she finished her wine, she would roll up her sleeves and her new life would begin.

Pincer and Tongue

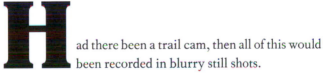

STEPHEN GRAHAM JONES

Had there been a trail cam, then all of this would been recorded in blurry still shots.

What happened had been centuries in coming. Rudolfo, the second vampire of his line and the oldest left anywhere on earth, had been lured into a daytime ambush deep in the Guatemalan jungle. He of course knew it could only be an ambush, and he also knew who the invitation had to have come from: Gretta, the German werewolf he had had a relationship with, each of them feeling the other's kind out, to see if this could even be a workable thing. The wrongness made it more fun than it should have been. It had started out as information gathering, but then they ended up truly smitten with each other, until . . . they weren't. Instead of going their separate ways and taking pains to stay out of each other's territory, however, well—they were exes. This big final blowout was bound to happen sooner or later. South America would be as good a place for it as any.

Rudolfo, of course, knew Gretta would come alone. Unlike his kind, her kind had a scent so distinct it could be made out for miles around, by anyone with the nose to smell.

Rudolfo came alone because, well: pride. And who knew, right? Maybe this would just be the opening steps of another decades-long dance for the two of them. Gretta was unpredictable and irascible, but that served to make her a good counterbalance for Rudolfo's calm, reserved, supposedly (so she said) "aloof" presence.

The world would tremble were the two of them to walk it hand in hand again. It could be like the old days. Until it wasn't.

But, as these things work, not only was there no trail cam installed, hopeful of documenting a migrant jaguar or a rutting armadillo, also no trail cam could realistically have seen into the hearts or lives of this vampire, that werewolf. It could have trapped their fight on its memory card, though.

It was epic.

Gretta came at Rudolfo not with her claws out and her hair on, but with a slashing blade. He, of course, dodged it, but in dodging it he had to whip back fast enough to impale himself on a wooden spike Gretta had embedded in a tree specifically for him.

Then she brought her claws out.

Rudolfo peeled his lips back from his mouthful of fangs, extracting himself hand over hand from the off-center spike while she raked him to ribbons, even going so far this time as to sever the pinky and ring fingers of his right hand.

He slung them away, dived at her, and she, wily as ever, dashed into the sunlight, trying to lure him to his death, taking their fight out of what would have been the frame of the trail cam, had the trail cam been there.

What that trail cam would have been seeing after the fight moved on to a different part of the jungle was just . . . leaf litter. A tropical jungle readying itself for the afternoon shower. Bugs resuming their insectile duties, birds flittering and fluttering.

And, just at the corner of the frame, two severed vampire fingers.

Two fingers that were now . . . moving?

Yes. But not of their own volition. Rudolfo, with his next full meal, could easily regenerate those fingers, should he survive Gretta's onslaught. If not—either way, really—once the next day's noontime sun beamed down through the canopy and found those fingers, they would flicker into flame, smoke away into nothing. Nature takes care of its own.

But *now* those fingers were . . . not so much crawling as traveling by antback or ant column—both—to the cavernous mound deep in the jungle, technically past the focal length of the trail cam, had there been a trail cam.

Had the digital file been delivered to the right hands, though, then focus could be changed, zooms could be faked, images unblurred such that they resolved into a lone finger jammed now at the main entry to the mound.

This entry isn't made for boons of this size, so accommodations must be made. Slowly, particle by particle, the entryway is crumbled wider, and one finger points down to where it's going, then goes there. The second passes through just as easily.

At which point some time lapse would need to occur. Trail cams are designed not to constantly record, but to motion-activate. What this means is that the trail cam would have zero access to the unholy miracle taking place underground, inside that ant mound.

Before imbibing Rudolfo's volatile blood, these ants had already been blanketing acres of land on what felt like a whim, leaving only waste and emptiness in their wake. Now, two days later, when the first of the infected ants are surging up from their mound, they've metastasized to a darker color, night now being their favored province, and they're more desperate for sustenance than before, no longer following chemical trails here and there but swarming forward in a ravenous world-eating mass.

The trail cam *could* have snapped poorly focused shot after shot of this, but if it had been there to do that, then it also could have been lucky enough to catch snatches of Rudolfo and Gretta's epic private battle from two days before.

At one point in it, far from the frame of the trail cam, had it been there, Rudolfo slings Gretta through the trunk of a tree and into the open mouth of a den or burrow of sorts, disturbing the lone occupant of that den or burrow.

Gretta comes to with, first, Rudolfo squatting across from her, cleaning his nails, and second, something nuzzling her backside.

She whips her foreleg around and extracts the bothersome creature, bites into its back to color herself with its blood so as to show Rudolfo what he has coming, but before she can spill that blood, he's on her again, savaging her vulnerable belly.

She tosses the animal aside, loses herself to bloodlust once again.

Three desperate, unrecorded hours later, spent, Gretta latches her jaws on to the back of Rudolfo's head and breathes her last, her great weight and last bite enough to keep Rudolfo there until the sun finds them both, burns them together.

Such is love.

Hours after *that*, though, the motion that would have activated the trail cam is that animal Gretta had only bitten, not killed. It comes to screaming, thrashing, writhing.

It's infected with her blood, with her ferocity, with her hunger.

It cowboy-walked away, following its long nose.

It doesn't blink, just flicks its long tongue ahead of it, and so this anteater with a werewolf heart waded into the roiling mass of vampiric ants, Rudolfo and Gretta's love for each other raging on past their own deaths, and it doesn't matter in the end whether there was a trail cam to document any of this or not. In three months, there aren't any people left to watch it anyway, just an eternal battle covering the face of the globe, neither side winning but neither side quite losing either, and so life struggles on in its tooth-and-claw way—its *pincer-and-tongue* way—finding its own terrible balance.

The Mask, the Ride, the Bag

CHASE BURKE

The night I drove the Mask around this past spring was suffocating, the way humid nights can be in the South, and I was behind on my rent. But that name, "the Mask," came later, with the bloggers and talking heads and their giddy speculation about his identity. At the time, to me, he was just another rider with a mediocre rating, the last in that night's long line of drunk students. Nothing more than money, my small cut of the gig economy.

I pulled up to the curb outside the bar and flashed my lights. He was holding a large bag at his side, one of those insulated cooler bags meant for trips to warehouse stores. He was well dressed, but his clothes were dirty, like he'd been in a fight in a dive-bar bathroom. He swung the bag into the backseat, sliding in behind it. Something smelled bad. Too many fine fraternity brothers had thrown up in my car over the years, to the point that I kept barf bags in the backseat, like an airliner, so I knew the smell of puke on clothing. This was worse, sharper, like the acidic tinge of rotting oranges.

"Riverside Apartments?" I said. He had requested six stops; this was the first.

YES, he said.

I froze. I felt his voice in my head and around me, echoing, like I was listening to multiple speakers playing the same sound milliseconds apart.

GO, he said.

I drove.

I glanced at him in the rearview as I neared Riverside, the student-condo complex by the fake lake next to the football stadium. His hair hung in front of his downcast face like the ribbons of a torn curtain.

I parked near the entrance. He shifted and eased open the door.

WAIT.

He extended an arm between the front seats. He clutched a wad of crumpled bills in a hand smeared with grime. The car's overhead light, dim as it was, took half the color out of everything.

YOU.

I hesitated. "But you're already paying through the app."

FOR YOU.

I had to pull the money from his half-clenched fist. He didn't have any fingernails.

He stared at the rearview, his face hidden in shadow. I couldn't shake the feeling that the shadow hid an empty space, blank skin, where eyes should be.

He stepped out of the car and leaned toward my window, gripping the roof where the door was open. I heard the creak of stressed plastic and metal, felt the car shift as he applied pressure.

WAIT.

He took more money from his bag, held it where I could see it in the parking-lot light. I nodded, and he walked toward Riverside. I understood.

He'd given me at least a hundred dollars. I stuffed it in one of the empty backseat barf bags, then wiped my shaking hands on a drive-thru napkin. Who *was* this person? I brought up his passenger profile, but it was blank. Before, there'd been a name, a face. Or had I imagined that? I tried to close the app and restart it, but my phone froze on the list of destinations. Five to go. I could do the math. I waited.

He returned after ten minutes, walking quickly, the bag over his shoulder bouncing against his leg with new weight. I wondered what he'd taken, and from whom. When he got in the car, the smell returned with him, stronger. He reached forward again, passing me another handful of money.

GO.

And that was how the next few hours went. I drove; I waited; I bagged damp and crumpled bills. I didn't ask questions. His bag grew bigger, distended. Every time he reached forward from the backseat his hands were dirtier, the grime thicker.

And the smell—god, the smell. When I was a kid, my brother and I found a run-down shed in the woods behind our grandfather's house, on someone else's rural Florida land. My brother, two years older, dared me to go inside. I pushed the door, then gagged, stumbling backward. Light cut through the doorway across the still form of a dead dog, its eyes open and covered in flies.

By the last stop, an apartment complex outside town adjacent to the river, I was living, fully, in that memory.

He heaved the bag into the footwell when he returned. It bulged like the stomach of an engorged animal.

DONE.

I kept my hands on the steering wheel, my eyes forward. *LOOK.*

His voice was like an arena of voices. He opened the bag, and I turned around.

At first I couldn't tell what was inside. The contents, nearly colorless in the weak light, glistened. But then I recognized in the amorphous red the metal wiring of braces around a full set of teeth, and the picture pieced together, the parts filled out into wholes. I vomited onto the floor.

YOU SEE.

He closed the bag and dragged it out of the car. He

tapped at my window, leaving a smear on the glass, until I rolled it down. My legs had cramped with fear. He held out more money. I could see his face for the first time: the haggard, pockmarked face of a young man like me. The bright ball of the streetlight reflected like white suns in his eyes. I took the cash.

He lifted the bag and swept his hair back in a single motion. When he looked at me again he was someone else, the face, impossibly, a reflection of my own. I was looking at myself. When he smiled, it was my smile, replaced with blackened teeth.

He walked down the street toward the river, dragging the bag behind him. He paused, once, to wave at me. His face had changed again.

The next day, the apartment murders were all over the news: six sleeping students pulled apart in different ways, their missing fingers, missing eyes, missing teeth. Most of a week went by with nothing but rampant speculation, stories running wild, before the police got two tips. Each said they saw a man carrying a bag through an apartment building's long hallway, and when he looked at them they said he changed his face, like he was taking off a mask.

It's been two months, and the summer is quiet. I needed to keep driving, but I couldn't do it, I couldn't even get in the car. I sold it a few weeks ago. The bag of cash sits untouched in a box in my closet. I try not to think about it, but I have to spend it soon. I'm broke. I don't leave my apartment much, and when I do, I avoid looking at people. I don't want anyone to see me. I don't want my face to be remembered, or recognized.

My brother called today, just to say hello. He asked how the driving life has been treating me, what with the slowdown of summer, the college town emptied of students who might never move back. Great, I said. Just great. It's a good way, I told him, to fake a living.

Cedar Grove Rose

CANISIA LUBRIN

They say Rose was born in invisible space. And because of this Rose could bend anything to her will. If you come upon the thick blockades of unbothered bush that surround Here, her neighborhood formed by the momentary rage of a volcano that no one remembers, nowadays you would have a bitch of a time convincing anyone of Rose's storied animalities. Here's one field with its pickets on the boundary still drawing apart sunlight and moonlight like matchsticks in the dirt. The sinewed edge of Here was once the British Empire's communications headquarters and its stronghold of slave catchers. And army whores during the Second World War. All the bays on the Atlantic side of Here are deep, just wide enough to keep ships unseen by enemy vessels. There has always been more here, of course. Rose knew this. But what nobody knows is that Rose made this invisible space of hers with all of its merciless things, that Rose turned a fugitive from There, a helloid by nearly any standard, into a Rose simply because she could.

Part of Rose's magic was how she ran. She ran often, faster than she really could, churning the earth-lain dirt into wings, or some dragonfly nebula. Almost made me wish I never gave up that job at the butterfly conservatory of There. In Rose's presence all of a pre-life leaped from its latency. She could bend time and man just the same. In a more just world, her unmarked grave would read: Here lies Haggard Rose, her life was the best and strangest alchemy.

Rose's mama would tap a metal spoon on the tar drum outside her kitchen when she needed her to do something, like chase down a chicken for dinner. Rose heard this tapping from miles out and would take to beating her feet along the roadside, making it home in record time, each time. But I want to tell you something particular about Rose and a stranger, a fella who seemed to be connected with a spoon in a way nobody out There has ever seen. I won't tell you how I know Rose and all this; we just don't have the time for that now. But you've got to believe me because I own these words.

This field was a big place, even to a kid like Rose, and she treated it like her own yard. Everything Here was miles between trees and something somebody threw away. Rose chased one rooster for two hours but it seemed he got smart and learned all her moves. Then the fella I told you about earlier, standing on the corner, called out to Rose, said his name was Baron, and that Rose should leave that chicken alone and let it "forget-about-you for a minute." Something was familiar about that fella all the same: his leathery face and the notebook he carried in a custom-made leather strap diagonal on his chest. His arms seemed attached a few inches too low from his shoulder blades. Then he pulled out a spoon from his back pocket and stuck it above his ear like a pencil. He was standing next to a big wooden tray with a small radio on it, and he had a pair of tap shoes strung over his bony shoulders.

"You're not from Here," Rose was saying to the fella.

"Well, if I'm Here, must be something here," he answered, but looking at me.

"Must be what thing," I cut in, knowing that there was nothing Rose ever came upon that did not suggest something else. Once when she fancied herself a musician, the pots and the pans, the potty with the broken lip, everything capable of making a hollow sound was an invitation to express her world-class musicianship. She even had a banana stand in for a violin one time and used her mama's bread knife as a bow. Her body, always Cartesian, turned things inside out. Even though she did not have the benediction of the church as a performer of miracles, this is what everybody knew. I was interested in this stranger, how he ended up Here. The Second World War was over and I was hellbent on mercy, not mercy really, but making sure to remind the brokers of mercy that they were not to actually claim its power. I had stopped a crowd from stoning a woman they thought was the wrong kind of whore. They ran me out of that town. I don't mind. I remember a time when Rose would have been hanged and burned for the things she can do, but that bygone era was one she herself willed out of existence. It has nothing to do with how many nails I have pulled out of my palms and feet.

So that fella, he had big crisscrossed teeth and a bad spotty beard, like Miss Mona's mangy dog. And when he smiled he looked deep into you and you knew things were about to go all green, that he saw things in you that you were afraid of just because you didn't know them yet. Things he had done, a horrible chronicle. Still, his little square mustache must have been the worst thing about him. That and how he looked to have leather skin, like it was grown in a lab to look dark and stay hard.

The fella had a dog with him. The dog had a crescent scar on its face like it had collided with a horse.

"Hey, kid," he said, "never mind what I am. Just say a word. Anything that a-come to mind."

Then Rose looked at him strange like he was stupid and Rose was smart, and the man said again, "Go on, now."

"Spoon," Rose said, stepping back. I know, but assume Rose didn't know what she was up to.

The man raised his arms slowly and arched himself into the shape of a goddamn spoon.

"Go on, another. Like . . . A color this time." The fella hacked through a laugh.

"Red," Rose said, wanting the man to melt this time.

The fella opened his arms like they were wings and brought his head down to his crotch. Then he twisted and turned himself until his head was sticking out from the middle of his body, now curved like a helix. He actually looked like a rose. It was disgusting, of course. Rose smiled. The fella looked horrified.

"One, two, three, four, five, six, seven, eight, nine . . . I'm coming!" he yelled, seemingly out of his own sense. The fella's voice was bubbly and jazzy in that kind of rusty way. I thought he was talking to me but he jumped, skipped a high skip over to the side, and started shuffling his feet and tapping and swirling his hand around his chest and his head and smiling. Then the dog jumped up on the table and pressed his little paw on the play button and on came some jazz. Some Coltrane. It must have been "Venus" but fifteen years too soon. And he did this counting and dancing for a time and then asked Rose to join him.

Well, Rose looked as though she didn't want anyone seeing her doing things with this lunatic but she broke off two sticks from the hibiscus plant on the left and started whipping the air, playing air drums. All the loud noises you wouldn't believe. It was, after all, that one night in 1938 that Rose's mama found her reputation as a Seeyer for being one of those women that warned the world about the end of the war. She was prone to happiness and unrepentant. "Take your shadow out and bury it if you won't let me do my work," she had told the local priest. Yet everyone criticized Rose roaming Here like she owned Here, making of her years some kind of failed psalmody, forgetting her mother's diatribe against the priest. But remember now that Rose was born in invisible space.

"Hey, mister!" Rose shouted through the commotion she had no doubt created. But he didn't seem to care to break from all his ticking about to look back at the girl. By a flash of sun off three brass teeth in the front of the fella's mouth, I had to look away quickly. In that brief time, I gleaned his hand. Its three and a half fingers. Rose's mama had told about the men who would come with the three and a half fingers and the notebooks filled with formulas for poisons and bombs and all manner of hell on earth. She had told of the submarines nestled in the Caribbean Sea and their torpedoes.

Rose shouted again, "Hey, mister!"

He turned back this time, weary as I'd ever seen a man who knew he had been eclipsed into exile.

#MOTHERMAYHEM

JEI D. MARCADE

Elodie Kang was in the shower when the skin of her right hand sloughed off.

She thought at first that she'd dropped her washcloth. One moment, she was working conditioner into her hair, and the next, she heard a wet slap against the bottom of the tub.

Elodie squinted at the bare bones that protruded from the smooth nub of her wrist. There was no pain. Though they had been stripped of flesh and muscle, the ends of each phalange remained as snugly joined as ever, and curled obediently when she clenched her fist.

"Eomma," she shouted. Panic lent a sharp edge to her voice.

A rush of footsteps on the stairs. Elodie's mother

barreled into the bathroom. She had been in the middle of lunch. Belatedly, Elodie grabbed for the towel and wrapped it around herself without stepping from under the showerhead.

"What? What happened?" Mrs. Kang cried in Korean. Her eyes flew to Elodie's hand, and the alarm faded from her features. "Finally. Thank God. Why are you just standing there? Turn off the water. Are you just going to let that clog the drain?"

Mrs. Kang reached past her daughter to scoop the soggy clump of subcutaneous tissue from the bottom of the tub with her chopsticks.

Elodie recoiled. "Eomma! That's so gross!"

Her mother made a dismissive sound as she slung it into the trash. "It's just skin. Now finish up and get dressed. I want to take pictures of your new hand to show Halmeoni."

Elodie had trouble sleeping. Not just because she had to get used to her bones snagging on the bedsheets or tangling in her hair.

The world made too much noise. Her bedroom walls and window panes might as well have been paper. Every slam of a car door or bark of a neighbor's dog sparked against her nerves.

She tried counting down from a thousand. She tried reciting her French vocabulary list. She listened to a true crime podcast about serial killers while she lay in bed with her eyes closed, and barely woke up in time for the bus.

•

You weren't allowed at school barehanded. If you didn't have gloves at home, you could pick a pair out from the bin in the main office, but those were bulky and unfashionable, and smelled like wet dog.

Elodie's grandmother had sent her a whole pack three years ago, delicately patchworked from silk hanbok scraps. The vibrant colors made Elodie self-conscious, and of course Kamryn noticed immediately.

"El-o-*die*," they squealed so loudly that Elodie winced. They turned her wrist to admire the elaborate embroidery at the cuff. "You got your *hand*? Why didn't you text me?"

Elodie felt like everyone in the hall was staring. She pulled away and mumbled a vague excuse, but Kamryn had stopped listening.

"Have you seen the Mother Mayhem challenge yet? The group chat's been blowing up about it all morning."

She hadn't. She'd turned off the notifications a while ago, unable to keep up.

Kamryn shoved a phone in Elodie's face. The video was dark, grainy, the focus trained on somebody's skeleton hand as it dangled off the edge of their bed in an unlit room.

It felt oddly transgressive to see a stranger's hand ungloved. As though she had glimpsed someone naked. Elodie tried to imagine filming herself like that, uploading it for the world to watch, and her cheeks burned.

A boy's voice murmured, "Mother Mayhem, grant me a boon." The pale, twig-like fingers closed.

The view distorted, jagged edges of static lancing across the frame.

When the boy opened his hand, a spiral shell lay cupped in the cage of his metacarpals.

"It's just a camera trick," Elodie said, but her voice was uncertain even to her own ears.

"It's not," Kamryn insisted. Anyway, now you can try it."

Last year, in the boys' locker room, some of the varsity football players had held down a couple of the JV kids, bone to skin. One fought free and ran for the assistant coach, but it was already too late.

Usually, it took a while for the effect to kick in, but with so many of them, only a few seconds of direct contact had made the other kid pass out. And then he'd dropped into a coma.

Someone from the student council had passed around a get-well card for him in homeroom, which Elodie had dutifully signed. The other guys were expelled. There had been a huge deal about it in the local papers, though it didn't make the national news; things like that happened too often for most of the major networks to care.

The kid woke up a couple months later, but never returned to school. Word was that he'd come back funny, that he saw things that weren't there.

Word was that he'd started the Mother Mayhem challenge.

•

Here are the rules: at the stroke of midnight, reach your skeleton hand into wherever the dark seems deepest. Common candidates are under the bed, in your closet— classic childhood monster haunts. Then you say the words, close your hand, and hold your breath until 12:01.

(There are variations. You must be the only person awake in your house. You must have a full-length mirror behind you. You must be wearing the same clothes, down to your underwear, for three days before the challenge.)

When you relax your fist, you'll find inside it a clue to how or when or where you'll die.

Elodie lost track of how many times she replayed that first video. She wondered what she'd do if she opened her hand to find a seashell resting there. Avoid beaches for the rest of her life? Skip out on post prom, which always took place on a yacht? She'd rather die.

At lunch, in study hall, behind the stairwell during passing period, her classmates traded their deaths. Drowning was preferred to burning. Falling was the crowd favorite for a while, until Shivam from Elodie's forensics club pulled an uncut emerald that got everyone guessing. A collapsed mine? A botched heist? At the end, he swapped it for a lipstick that he insisted meant *assassination by femme fatale*, which they all agreed would be a pretty hot way to go. Way better than sticking around for the end of the world.

Elodie did the Mother Mayhem challenge, of course.

It was inevitable, from the first time she punched in the hashtag on her own phone and watched dozens of skeleton hands unfurl like bony flowers in bloom around shell casings and car keys and the plastic caps to syringes.

She did the challenge—repeatedly.

Night after night, Elodie called on Mother Mayhem and plucked from the air and darkness ticket stubs and ball bearings and, once, a spool of thread. These she threw into a tea tin that she shoved underneath her bed. She thought she could hear them sometimes, all her little deaths rattling gently below her pillow like her own personal white noise machine, lulling her to sleep.

Leg

BRIAN EVENSON

The captain of the vessel was named Hekla, a name that in the language of her ancestors meant "cloak," though she had never worn a cloak. One of her legs was not a leg at all but a separate creature that had learned to act like a leg. When she needed to walk about her vessel this served as a leg for her, but once she was alone in her quarters she would unstrap it and it would unfurl to become a separate being, something she could converse with, a trusted advisor, a secret friend. Nobody knew it to be other than an artificial leg except for her.

Hekla had found the leg before she became captain, a few moments after she lost her flesh-and-blood leg, severed cleanly mid-thigh in a freak accident. Hekla had the presence of mind to tourniquet what was left of her thigh. She

BRIAN EVENSON

was fading from consciousness, having lost too much blood, when it appeared.

It was bipedal but strange and glittering, made of angles and light. Each time Hekla looked at it, it seemed subtly different.

"What is that?" asked the creature.

"What?" Hekla managed.

"The dark substance puddling around you."

"That is my blood," said Hekla. "I will soon die."

"Ah," said the creature.

"You don't exist," claimed Hekla. "I'm hallucinating you."

The creature ignored this. Instead it said, "Would you not prefer to live?"

And with this began a relationship that bound Hekla and leg tightly together.

"I'm bored," she told the leg one day many years later, once she was captain of a vessel. "We do nothing but float. I want something exciting to do."

The leg told her this: "On the winds of the darkness is a creature as long as this vessel, and which moves in a slow undulating pattern across the currents of space. Its back is quivered with spines and it is long and thin like a snake but has the head and metal-breaking bill of a bony fish. With a swipe of its tail it could destroy this vessel."

"Why do you tell me this, leg?" she asked.

Leg shrugged. "It is a worthy foe. I thought you might like to hunt it."

At first Hekla dismissed leg's suggestion out of hand. It made no sense to endanger her crew and the passengers sleeping in the storage pods for her own amusement. But as the days dragged slowly past, she began to favor the idea.

Eventually she listened to the leg with interest. When it told her where such a creature was most likely to be found, she directed the navigator to change course.

"Why should I change course?" he asked. His name was Michael.

"Because I am your captain," said Hekla. "And I tell you to do so."

"We have a destination," said Michael. "A new life awaits us."

"Change course," said Hekla.

"I will not change my course without a reason," said Michael.

So Hekla explained.

"This is not a worthy reason," said Michael once she was finished. "If you do this thing, many of us will die, perhaps even all of us. No, I will not alter our course. We shall continue to our intended destination."

The captain asked again, and again he refused. In the end he made it clear that she would have her way only if she killed him first.

She returned to her quarters muttering to herself, "What use is it to be captain if I cannot have my way?"

Once back in her quarters, she released her leg. It unfurled and revealed itself.

"Did you hear him, leg?" she asked.

The leg simply inclined its head—for as curious as it seems, the leg, when unfurled, had a head—to indicate that it had.

"Who is the captain?" asked the leg in its strange voice. "Is it not you?"

"It is indeed me," said Hekla.

"Then force him to do it," the leg said.

"He claims he would rather die first," said Hekla.

"Then kill him."

But the captain did not want to kill Michael herself. She knew it was wrong and that she would feel guilty doing so. And yet, perhaps if she were not the one to do the actual killing, it would not be as wrong and she would be able to live with what had been done. The only one she could trust to kill Michael and keep her involvement a secret was leg.

"Leg," she said.

"Hekla," said leg, and bowed deeply.

"Will you kill Michael for me?"

"Yes," said leg. "Here is what we will do. You will go to the navigation center when he is alone and you will secure the door from within. When he asks you what you are doing, you will ignore him and release me and I will unfurl and kill him."

"I do not want to be there when he dies," said Hekla. "I do not want to see it or for anyone to guess I am involved. Find another way."

Leg thought.

"Take me off in your room. Then I will unfurl, walk down the corridor, enter the navigation center, and kill him."

"People will see you walking and see what you are and they will shriek and scream. No one must know I have you, leg. If they realize you are more than a leg, they will destroy you, and perhaps me as well. Think again, leg."

Leg thought long.

"I will change myself," said leg finally. "I will take on your countenance and in that guise I will kill him."

"Can you do this?" said Hekla, amazed. "Can you become just like me?"

"Yes, and act like you, too. But only if you grant me permission."

And so Hekla did.

As she watched, leg underwent a transformation, taking on first her height and figure and then the specifics of her features. In the end there was nothing to tell the two of them apart except that the captain was missing her prosthetic, and leg, in becoming captain, had thought to give itself what seemed an artificial leg.

When Hekla looked upon this perfect replication of herself, she felt a shiver run through her.

"Go," she said. "Kill him."

"I go," said leg, and left.

Leg went through the door and out into the passageway. It walked slowly toward the navigation center, where Michael was. This was the first time it had been out of the captain's quarters on its own. This was the first time it had been away from the captain since leg had found her. Leg enjoyed how this felt.

Leg arrived at the navigation center. Michael was there, and alone.

"It's no use trying to convince me," said Michael. "I won't change my mind."

"I'm not going to try to convince you," said leg, and killed him. To do this, leg turned itself inside out and engulfed him, so that the blood, when it came spattering forth, would be hidden inside. Then leg released the exsanguinated body and turned itself right side out again. Inside, it was spattered with Michael's blood. On the outside, the false Hekla looked clean and untouched.

And so leg killed Michael and left his body on the floor. Then it bent over the body and stared at it long and hard. Slowly it took on the shape and form of Michael, for once someone was dead, leg did not need their permission to become them.

Leg went back to the captain. At first she thought it to be Michael, since Michael was who it resembled. The captain drew back as leg came closer, afraid, until the moment when

Michael's features began to smooth out and leg became itself again. Then it folded up tightly and became her leg again, though now it was aslosh inside with a dead man's blood. Wherever the captain walked, she heard it.

And after? Some believe that, once Michael was dead, leg was satisfied to remain as it was, hidden, the captain's confidant. Others believe that leg acquired a taste for being human and did not want to give this up. At night, while the captain slept, it would take on her form or that of Michael and wander the ship. Occasionally, as a special treat, it would turn itself inside out and kill someone, and then it would dispose of the body, sometimes jettisoning it into space, other times incinerating it with a mechanism incorporated into its body. There are those who say that by the time the vessel reached the vast creature Hekla intended to hunt, leg had destroyed the crew manning the vessel and had begun on the passengers suspended in the storage pods. Only the captain and leg were left awake and alive, and soon the ship was destroyed and the captain killed.

And leg? Soon it reached its mature form and became snake-bodied with the head of a bony fish, as it had always been meant to do. It is no doubt out there still, swimming alone along a current of darkness.

Veins, Like a System

ESHANI SURYA

The doctor stands at the sink, filling a syringe with oil, viscous and strangely red-black. Finally, the liquid reaches the appropriate milliliter mark—a number Lane isn't privy to—and the doctor tips the needle back and forth, watching the oil slosh a little and settle. Lane tightens his fist, trying to coax the veins there to grow starker. This procedure, early petrochemical therapy, is a benefit, not yet available to the public, offered to employees of the oil company where Lane is a manager. He massages the skin at his inner elbow.

Are you sure about this? Lane's wife, Katherine, asks from her chair. She still has her coat on, and she twists a loose thread around her pointer finger.

It's perfectly safe, the doctor says, even though Katherine might have been asking Lane. He sterilizes

Lane's skin. *It'll stimulate everything, keep it all running. Especially the organs.*

Which organs? Lane asks.

Deep breath, the doctor instructs, and the needle jabs through the flesh. *Heart, lungs, eyes. You'll be able to see when you're saturated.*

Not in your eyes, Katherine says. *Lane, not eyes.*

It's part of the procedure, Lane says.

Oil is where the money comes from. It's how they buy their son, Ev, a new backpack when the old one is frayed, how they keep cut flowers on the dining room table instead of leaving the centerpiece empty. If there are lawsuits, the pelicans shaking their slick black feathers with despair, the whispers of colleagues in different states suffering from nausea, memory loss, Lane chooses not to play the poor fool cynic, too bitter and missing out.

A few months later, Lane and Ev play basketball in the cracked driveway, weak spring sun traversing their spines. Ev dribbles through his legs and swishes past his father to score a layup, but Lane thinks of a recent pipeline fracture around Lubbock. A gelding took off by leaping across a fence, and when they found him in the long corridor of a corn field, they pried his teeth open for the bit and found his tongue all inky shine, an ominous rainbow in black from drinking water at the stream. No choice, they put the poisoned horse down, and Lane wonders how much the creature could've ingested, if it was any more than the milliliters the doctor slips into his bloodstream every week.

Just then, Ev barrels at him, elbow flailing, but Lane sidesteps and dodges the blow. His body locks, tensing for disaster, and doesn't relax.

Idiot, Lane cries out, grabbing Ev's collar and shaking him with fury.

Dad, Ev says, slowly wedging his fingers in the tight spaces between his father's digits. He looks away from Lane's gaze—he has been nervous ever since the veins in Lane's eyes turned black from the oil treatments. *What are you doing?*

Lane isn't usually prone to anger, but he understands his body as weaker now, even if it thrums with energy. What runs through him is volatile, not meant to spill out of the web into the rest of the cells. The safety he believed in before is tenuous. Slowly, he steps back, straightens his son's shirt at the shoulder blade, and retreats to the house.

It takes less than purposeful violence to empty a vein, just him dressing for church, while Ev complains about hating the preacher. It's then, as Lane agitatedly pulls clothes from his closet, that a belt buckle smacks into his eye. Searing pain blacking out his vision, and then he realizes that it's not just that, but oil leaking out, dripping down his cheek. He touches it again and again, smearing it around in his soft under-eye region. Someone pulls him along urgently.

Don't look, Ev, Katherine says, closing the bathroom

door. She positions Lane under the light and tries to open his lids wider, but he winces. The half of his face covered in oil is burning, like the skin is freckling into a thousand sores.

Katherine wets the cloth under some water and presses it to his face, but it doesn't help. His eye is hot and somehow it doesn't seem as solid. Like pudding on a stove, like jelly mixed hard with a spoon. He can't see right, his vision teeters, unbalanced.

You should look at yourself, Katherine says. *You should see what you let them do.*

In the mirror, he has only one eye. The other is a dark, empty space, the inside burned away. He is raw, he is forever changed. When he looks back at Katherine, he sees that Ev has come inside anyway, though he hides his face in his mother's blouse. She is crying.

No one told him about these close-up consequences of a leak. Maybe the Lubbock ground aches too, the gelding just the visible harm. Lane wonders if they'll have to put him down now. When he looks at his family's faces, fighting the dizziness latched on like a mask over his mouth and nose, he understands what Katherine meant that first day when she begged him to spare his eyes. Once the three of them owned the looks between them; no longer.

Caravan

PEDRO INIGUEZ

Rudy raised his arm and wiped the sweat from his brow. Around him, thousands of people from the caravan settled into the Zócalo in Mexico City. Here and there, volunteers wove their way through the crowd, dispensing food, medical aid, and clothes.

A light-skinned boy named Enrique who'd traveled in Rudy's immediate clique received a pristine Cruz Azul cap from a generous woman. She caressed his face and made friendly chatter with his father, Guillermo, the fat man from Honduras. Rudy looked at his own arms. They were dark, and shimmering with sweat. A group of curious onlookers gave them cold stares, as if looking upon a herd of animals.

Rudy's mother pulled him close. "Mijo, stay close. Stray children have been known to get snatched here."

Rudy turned his head to look up at her.

"This world is full of monsters. They kidnap children and demand ransoms or sell their organs on the black market. We're not in Guatemala. People disappear here all the time."

"Monsters?" Rudy asked. He wanted to ask what she meant but he knew better than to question his mother.

They walked inside a large tent and received the best meal he'd had in weeks, since crossing the border into Chiapas: a bowl of rice, beans, corn, and tortillas.

"Enjoy," his mother said. "It only gets harder from here."

The nights were the worst for Rudy. He sat beside himself and wrapped his arms across his chest and shivered in front of the campfire. He looked at the people around him as the light danced across their bodies. Their faces looked gaunt and pale, like corpses. Many had grown thin, relying on the generosity of strangers for food. He'd spotted some of the men catching rats and bashing them against rocks and grilling them over the open flames.

Some of the older travelers stayed behind to wither away as their feet could no longer carry them.

Tonight, they camped outside San Miguel, Sinaloa. His mother had left for town to scavenge for dinner. She often left him alone at night, as she offered her services to old townsfolk or to local butchers who detested cleaning the bloody counters and allowed her to do it in return for scraps.

As he waited for his mother to return, he made a game of counting the people in his clique. He counted fifty. The group had thinned out over the last month. Many of them disappeared during the night. Some, he'd overheard, had turned back as the trip dragged on and food became scarce. Others sought asylum in the small towns they'd ventured through, choosing to start anew in Mexico. Sometimes he'd even hear parents crying on about their children vanishing, pleading for anyone to help start a search party. Most people ignored the pleas and carried on. That's why his mother didn't let him make friends with any of the other children; it would hurt too much if you didn't see them again.

Rudy wondered about the monsters his mom had mentioned. They couldn't be real, could they?

He tried not to think about it. There was a rational explanation for their losses. Some people had chosen to travel another route. That was it. After the caravan disembarked the freight train in Guanajuato, half the group splintered and traveled north, hoping to enter through Texas. Mother had said the cartels were worse in that part of Mexico. Maybe they were the real monsters . . .

Rudy's belly rumbled as it had for the last week, and he hoped his mother would come back soon.

He looked across the way and spotted Guillermo and his son, Enrique. Guillermo's shirt appeared tighter on him, as if he had gained weight over the last few days. Rudy wondered how the man had stayed so plump while everyone else starved. He was eating well, and Rudy hated him for it. He hated Enrique, too, for being given such a fancy new hat. He knew it was because dark people like him were seldom given anything but mean stares.

Rudy's mom suddenly approached the camp. She smiled at him and placed two slabs of meat onto a pan and set it down over the fire.

"I helped the owner of another butcher shop clean down his counters," she said. "I think I'm on to something."

The sizzle of the meat had stirred a few curious onlookers who soon returned to their starved slumber.

After dinner Rudy slept well and dreamed of the promise of a new country.

They'd crossed the Sonoran Desert and headed farther north, where they now made camp in the Tijuana countryside, just outside a colony of concrete-and-sheet-metal huts. There were just twenty people in the group. His mother had been right; people disappeared in this country left and right.

Rudy crouched alone beside the campfire where his mother had told him to wait. He dwelled on the border, now just a half day's walk away.

Guillermo buried his face in his hands and sobbed beside Rudy. Enrique had vanished as evening came, and Rudy couldn't help but feel guilty. Maybe if they'd been friends, they could've watched over each other.

"My son is gone," Guillermo said. "Will no one help me find him?"

"You have nothing to cry about, you monster," shouted one of the women. "We know you've been snatching children in the night and slaughtering them to keep yourself fed."

"No, I, I don't know what you're talking about."

"That's right," said an old man. "We've been talking about it. Interesting how all of us are starving, yet you keep getting fatter. How do you explain that?"

The rest of the adults in the group stood and surrounded Guillermo. One of the men pulled on his collar. Rudy stood and stepped away. He hoped his mother would hurry back.

"No, wait, I can explain." Guillermo reached for his wallet. "Look," he said, retrieving a wad of cash. "In Honduras I was a wealthy man. I've been buying food."

"And you didn't think to share with us. When so many of us were starving?" the woman said.

The group hauled him off into the darkness of the countryside until Rudy could no longer see them. Guillermo's screams faded after a while.

Rudy smiled as his mom returned from Tijuana. He'd never felt so relieved.

As always, she returned with two thin strips of meat. One for her and one for him. She slapped them on the pan over the fire and brought Rudy against her body.

"Tomorrow a new life begins for us," she said. She

retrieved something from a small plastic bag. "I found you this hat, Mijo. I think you'll like it."

She placed a Cruz Azul hat on his head. The hat was crumpled and a little wet with something, but felt warm in the bitter, cold night.

Downpour

JOSEPH SALVATORE

The rat had been trapped on the subway platform for a half hour before Rose lugged the dripping baby stroller down the stairs to the swamp of bodies waiting in the humidity for the L train to Manhattan. The sudden July downpour brought even more riders than usual off Bedford Avenue and down to the trains. And when Rose finally got down there, Emma was miraculously still asleep. Rose put the brake on the carriage and thought about opening the plastic rain cover, but when she saw her four-month-old's sleeping face, she decided to keep her inside her plastic bubble.

Rose turned to see a swath split the crowd, parting them like a zipper, everyone jumping and lifting their legs and holding on to other people. The woman in front of Emma's stroller screamed, "Fucking rat!" Rose saw the

JOSEPH SALVATORE

rat dart under a bench and then reemerge on the other side
and scurry under a trash barrel, its long gray tail twitching
like a dying worm. A white girl with dreadlocks and de-
signer bell-bottoms screeched and jumped up on the bench,
clutching her backpack to her chest and laugh-whining to
her friends, still standing around her. Someone called for
help, at which point—*deus ex machina*—a cleaner in dark
blue subway overalls came down the stairs with a broom
the size of a hammerhead shark, with bristles as big as chopsticks. He silently moved into the crowd, laser-focused on
finding the rat. He held the broom up with two hands and
approached the trash barrel stealthily, as everyone moved
back, crowding Rose and the stroller closer to the edge of
the platform.

The cleaner crept toward the barrel with the broom
raised like a spear. The rat's tail disappeared under the barrel and everyone let go a collective groan. Suddenly the
man released the broom, throwing it like someone trying
to spear a buffalo. When the broom stopped, the rat rolled
out from under the bristles, not dead but moving much more
slowly than it had been for the last half hour. Some of the
crowd whooped and others gasped. The man picked up
the broom and the rat rolled over quickly, and the people
moved back again, this time forcing the stroller's handle
into Rose's belly, and just then she saw the red light of a
subway train growing larger inside the tunnel. She felt the
breeze of its approach and swung the stroller out and away
from the edge. But the rat leaped up, the crowd surged back

again, and the man plunged the broom at it once more, not throwing it this time, but stabbing it, stunning the rat, now lying flat on its belly, a rear leg out at an angle impossible to believe didn't indicate a break.

Someone shouted for the man to stop, to leave it alone now. Rose joined the group and yelled for the man to sweep the poor thing onto the tracks. But her voice was drowned out by the arriving train.

As the doors opened, Rose gently tilted the stroller back over the lip of the car's floor and pushed to the other side, nestling it tight between the doors and the blue seat next to it. She used her foot to kick off the brake, leaned against the doors, and watched the man begin sweeping the dazed rat toward the platform's edge, pushing it hard and fast. Whether he heard Rose or not, she thought, he was doing just as she'd suggested.

It was then the rat leaped up again, as if it had been playing possum, electrified and wild, running between legs and luggage and jumping between the subway doors just as they were closing, a dark blur flying at knee level across the car. Rose looked down just in time to see the rat's tail disappear under the rain cover of the stroller, a dark shadow moving up and over Emma's body toward her face, a wild spray of red splashing across the plastic bubble. Emma's tiny pink-socked foot began to kick wildly, and Rose tore into the rain cover but could not puncture it, could not pull it off the stroller's frame. She pitched the whole thing over on its side and went up under it with her hands and head disappearing in the same spot the tail had disappeared moments ago.

Under the cover it was hot and wet, so much hotter and wetter than the Brooklyn afternoon out of which she and Emma had stepped in search of some relief.

Human Milk for Human Babies

LINDSAY KING-MILLER

MESSAGE REQUEST

From: Zuzu Shaw

To: Cori Kennedy

Hi Cori, I saw your post on the Mother's Milk forum about having oversupply and wanting to donate milk. I would love to take you up on your generous offer. I'd be happy to come by your house to pick it up.

If you respond to this message, Zuzu Shaw will be added to your list of contacts.

From: Cori Kennedy

To: Zuzu Shaw

Hi Zuzu! Wow, you responded to my post fast. Yes, I'd love to have you come pick up some milk and help me reclaim my freezer space, LOL! How old is your babe? Mine is starting to wean herself, but I have to keep pumping because every time I stop I get mastitis. UGH. We're up on the north side by the lake, how about you? Want to bring your little one with you? Amelie and I could both use a playdate! We just moved here right before she was born and we haven't really found our "people" yet.

From: Zuzu
To: Cori
I also live near the lake. How does 1 pm tomorrow sound? We don't have many people either, although we've been in this area longer.

From: Cori
To: Zuzu
Awesome! Here's my address: [open in map]

From: Zuzu
To: Cori
Thank you (and Amelie) for having me over today, and for sharing your milk. I'm sorry I couldn't bring my little girl with me, but I hope we can meet up again soon. After all, she and Amelie are milk sisters now, so in a way, we're all a family.

FRIEND REQUEST

To: Zuzu Shaw

Cori Kennedy has sent you a Friend Request. If you accept, you will be able to see and interact with each other's Profile.

From: Cori

To: Zuzu

Hey! I added you hoping I could peek at cute baby pictures on your profile, but I guess you're not as much of a paparazzi mama as me. Could you send me a pic of your little one, and remind me what her name is?

From: Zuzu

To: Cori

I worry about privacy with putting photos online. I have some on my phone but I lost my charger; I'll text you after I get a new one. In the meantime, do you happen to have any more milk you can spare?

From: Cori

To: Zuzu

Absolutely! Wow, she went through that fast. Is she hitting a growth spurt? Amelie just had one a few weeks ago, and they're right around the same age, aren't they? It's so wild how you wake up in the morning and they're like six inches longer than you remember. We're going to be out running errands today, so I can just bring a cooler by, since you're in the neighborhood. Can you send me your address?

From: Zuzu
To: Cori
They just keep growing and growing. Always hungry. Don't worry about dropping it off, I can pick it up another day.

From: Cori
To: Zuzu
It's no trouble! I'm already out and I have the cooler in my backseat, so I should really get it to you before it gets too warm.

From: Zuzu
To: Cori
I live here: [open in map] Please don't ring the doorbell, I don't want anything to wake up.

From: Cori
To: Zuzu
Thanks for taking the milk off our hands, and I'm sorry for interrupting you in the middle of a nap! Totally understand not letting us in, but I'd love to come over sometime when you're up to having company and the baby isn't asleep. I'll bring takeout and a bottle of wine, LOL.

From: Zuzu
To: Cori
Thank you for the invitation to Amelie's birthday party. We won't be able to make it that day, but congratulations to you both on a year of life.

From: Cori
To: Zuzu
No worries! I'm also using the birthday as an impetus to go through Amelie's dresser and putting together a box of things to give away. Your little one is younger, right? Do you want to look at stuff before we take it to Goodwill?

From: Zuzu
To: Cori
Thank you for the offer, but no, my child is older than Amelie.

From: Cori
To: Zuzu
Why did I think she was younger? It's so funny that after all this time I still haven't met your daughter! What are the two of you up to this weekend? We might go to the zoo.

From: Zuzu
To: Cori
May I come by and pick up more milk?

From: Cori

To: Zuzu

I was hoping to tell you this in person, but it's so hard to find time to meet! Now that Amelie is a year old, I'm trying to cut back on pumping and letting my supply dry up. I have a little bit in the freezer from the last few weeks, but after that I think I won't have milk to donate anymore. Hopefully we can still find occasional excuses to get together!

From: Cori

To: Zuzu

I saw your post on the forum asking for donor milk—you sound really panicked and I'm sorry for taking you by surprise! I didn't realize you were running so low. Pardon me for being intrusive, but your daughter must be eating solid food by now, right? It's probably not healthy for her to subsist on nothing but milk, if she's more than a year old.

From: Zuzu

To: Cori

It's not healthy at all.

From: Cori

To: Zuzu

Are you at home right now? Can I bring the last of my milk by, and maybe we can talk?

From: Zuzu
To: Cori
I'm not at home. I'm at the house.

From: Cori
To: Zuzu
I'm worried about you. Stay calm, okay? I'll be right over.

From: Cori
To: Zuzu
Are you here? I've been knocking on the door but no one is answering.

From: Cori
To: Zuzu
I hear someone crying inside. Is that you? Is it your daughter? If you don't answer the door I'm going to call somebody.

From: Zuzu
To: Cori
Don't leave. I can't do this without you. I tried to do it alone but it's just too hard.

From: Cori
To: Zuzu
Believe me, I understand. You don't have to be ashamed that you're struggling. I know how hard raising a baby alone is.

•

From: Zuzu
To: Cori
You don't know. But I'll show you. Stay there. I'm coming.

MISSING WOMAN SUSPECTED OF CHILD ABANDONMENT

Lakeview—Police are searching for Cordelia Kennedy, age 27, who is suspected of abandoning her 1-year-old daughter.

Kennedy, a single mother, has not been seen since she left work on the afternoon of Friday, August 25. Her daughter was found by police in a house several blocks from Kennedy's residence. Neighbors called police when they heard a child crying from inside the house, which has been unoccupied for more than a year.

Kennedy's car was found outside the house, but her phone and purse were gone. There was no sign of struggle. The child was unharmed and is in city custody while authorities attempt to find her other family members.

Pictures of Heaven

BEN LOORY

A man decides to paint a picture of Heaven—the idea just comes to him one night. So he goes out and buys a canvas and some paints.

And when the picture's done, it's all right.

There are angels with wings, and big white fluffy clouds, and lots of glowing halos, and a harp. And there's a man on a throne—an old man with a beard—who, one assumes, must be God.

And the man kind of likes it!

But then he tilts his head.

There's something about the picture that isn't right.

Hmm, says the man.

He stares at it awhile.

Then he takes a big brush and paints it white.

•

I'll do it again tomorrow and it'll be better, the man says.

He turns out the lights and goes to bed.

But for some reason, he can't sleep. He lies there in the dark.

Guess I'll do it better now, he finally says.

So the man gets out of bed and paints another picture. But this time, the picture is even worse. The halos are all crooked and God looks slightly crazed—like a hungry man trying to sell insurance.

Ugh, says the man, and takes a step back.

We'll try again tomorrow, he says.

He picks up the big brush and paints the canvas white.

And then he turns and goes back to bed.

It takes him a really long time to fall asleep, and when he does, it's no fun at all. He keeps dreaming that he's painting terrible pictures of Heaven.

Dammit, get it right! a voice calls out.

So at the crack of dawn, the man gets up and starts to paint again. He doesn't even have his coffee first.

I gotta get this picture done—and *done right!* he says.

But the third picture is infinitely worse.

•

This third picture doesn't look even a bit like Heaven. It's all a sickening, flickering shade of red. The angels look enraged, and a few are holding pitchforks.

And God isn't there—he's gone away.

Oh God, the man says.

He slashes up the canvas. He balls it up and shoves it in the trash. He breaks up all his brushes, pours the paints straight down the drain.

It's okay, he says. It's all alright!

I just have to not paint any more pictures, he says.

Okay, he says. Time to take a walk.

He opens up the front door and heads off down the street.

What a nice day! he says.

But something's off.

Yes, the sky is blue, and yes, the sun is out, and yes, there are birds in the air. And yes, there are couples walking past and kids at play.

But something's different—though what, he cannot say.

The man peers about—searching, squinting hard—and after a while, he starts to see: the passersby are regarding him with strange and furtive looks.

And he smells something burning on the breeze.

•

Smoke! the man thinks. Is there a fire somewhere?

He cranes his neck around, trying to see.

Somehow, the temperature seems to have risen.

The man reaches up and undoes his collar.

I don't think that loosening your collar's gonna help, a man passing by says, with a leer.

Strangely, this man appears to have a forked tail—and cloven hooves? That seem to clatter as he comes near?!

Oh God! the man yells.

He turns and runs away—straight into the midst of a swirling crowd.

They're all cackling at him—demons and devils!

He turns his eyes quickly to the ground.

Please, God, the man says, just let me get back home!

That prompts roaring laughter from all around.

The man claps his hands over his ears and turns and runs.

Once home, he locks the door and pulls the window shades all down.

The man hides in the bathroom.

What do I do, what do I do? he says.

Suddenly he remembers the painting.

It must be because of that, he thinks. I have to get it right! If I paint Heaven right, this nightmare will stop!

Okay! says the man, and claps his hands together.
    Then he remembers he poured his paints away.
    And the canvas, too, he thinks, is gone.
    He looks toward the door.
    But there's no way he's going out *there* to buy more.

And at that very moment, the walls begin to crack—and through the cracks, the man sees only fire.
    He tries to back away, but there's nowhere to go.
    Then two dark eyes appear inside the fire.

Well? says a voice.
    But how? says the man.
    These few moments left are all he's got.
    And suddenly the man laughs—and he paints a perfect Heaven.
    He does it on the floor, in his own blood.

Gabriel Metsu, Man Writing a Letter, c. 1664–66

HELEN McCLORY

So I'm not a docent now, but in my years in that field I became familiar with the idea that there are many paintings that have an atmosphere. Put it that way. I'm not talking about hyperactive eBay entries, ugly amateurish work that gets boosted by having a legend attached. I don't judge anyone for trying to keep their pockets lined in such a creative way. It's a kind of art in itself, in my view. But I'm speaking of *classical* works, with reputations that don't need that kind of thing to make them memorable. Ones you'd know in a second, or have a sense that you should, anyway. I have had the good luck to stare at many iconic paintings from my little stool, getting to know them really well, getting to understand each colored inch of them, and, another benefit, seeing how other people respond to them; silent appraisals, grunts and little gasps, funny comments, the movements folks will make trying to orient themselves to something they have seen a hundred times before in other, lesser frames. And some of these paintings, just a very few, have a different kind of presence.

Which paintings, you'll ask, haunted sunflowers? Or did the many heads of Marilyn start wheedling from that Warhol number? I know you're going to take it wrongly, on purpose. You don't believe in presences. You don't believe in *me*. But you're sitting with me, and listen—I'm only going to tell you about the one thing, and I'm not going to stutter. The ghost isn't a metaphor for my boredom, my depression, my failed marriage, or my bad left leg. I saw it, that's the truth.

I met him in the Smithsonian Gallery of Art, when he was on loan from Dublin. You can probably guess the setting for the encounter: late on, right as the gallery is closing up for the night, lights going off, and I'm putting my things away in the locker and hear a noise—come on. I'm a *docent*. I'm not in the building late, that's *security*. So it was early, before we opened. The morning was streaming in through the skylight. That particular gallery had been newly hung, mostly Vermeers. I want to make some joke about teeth, but I can't think of one right now. Teeth, Jesus. This was the first chance I'd got to look at him, and I was taking my time. I liked to do that, get a good first look fresh, before other people came between me and the work, with all their impressions rubbing over before I had the chance to make mine. So I went up before him and took my time. The man writing a letter is wearing some fantastic black silky coat and his white linen sleeves and neckline are all ruffles. There's a hat perched on his chairback. A painting on the wall behind him of an autumn countryside and animals. He has long, wavy fair hair and delicate features, looks about fourteen. You could say he'd be any gender. He's writing that letter on a desk by a window in the left part of the frame—I suppose that's why they put him with the Vermeers. That man loved a leftward window. The most beautiful part of the painting is the spectacular arrangement he's got for a tablecloth. It's opulent orange-reds and blues, looks like an antique carpet. He's a rich boy, my man. He looks like he might be writing a college admissions letter, though I know there's a companion piece to this, *Woman Reading a Letter*, so I guess it's something to her. His eyes are looking down and mostly closed.

At least, they were at first.

I'm not easily scared. You think I haven't seen things, working with the public so close for so long? I have seen the way folks behave when they think no one's watching, and I'm no one to them. That lesson I learn over and over. I've heard men howling, old men weeping, little kids hissing and walking backward from Francis Bacon pictures that crackle with malign intent. I've faced down Rothkos that pulled my soul half out like a string of flags from my throat. I have seen somebody try to stab themselves in front of Botticelli's *Venus*, and I was only at the Uffizi on *holiday*. I have seen paintings move before. Seen them jump off the wall when no one's touched them and the fittings are high-tensile backings installed months before. But I swear, I stood in front of *Man Writing a Letter*, a peaceful painting, in high actual daylight and watched his fingers *start to move* his white quill over the page.

I could hear the sounds from the street outside. The street outside the painting. Carts rolling. A dog. People carrying on lives that were not there. I looked at the globe behind him and saw how papery yellow it looked, like a skull. I saw the thick red of the tablecloth so clearly I could have been feeling the grain of it myself, with my own fingers. All this, could be I was imagining it, yes, caught up in the details, getting a little lost in them. I stood and allowed myself to believe that. I've seen masterpieces that can do almost as much, like I said. But just as I was going to make my turn to the stool, to look for the first folks coming by, I saw him move his whole head and look at me.

He opened his mouth. Sweet mouth it is. I was terrified by its sweetness, and I saw his small teeth, which were wet, which nobody's ever seen, and he put the pen down, and *got up*. The length of him, standing in his black frock coat and trousers, white shirt. He moved forward a little—the painting is close in on him, he had so little distance he could go.

He plucked his hat off the back of the seat and put it on his head. He was getting ready to get down.

Then I don't know what he did, because I got myself out of there.

Of course I had to go back to work after a little bit. You think I just ran out on a good docent job? I stayed my distance from him, glad when the room was chock-full of people, all looking at girls pouring milk from jugs. From across the room I kept him in my indirect line of sight. Paintings demand an emotional response from you, some more than most. Part of it is the quality of the work, part knowing how much *older* they are than you. That boy who is a man is three hundred and fifty-odd. Time enough for him to grow a self, and use it, when he can. Maybe I was just tired, you'll say, thinking a painting looked at me. With the idea, maybe, that I've felt invisible in this line of work. Maybe no, I say. It was him that was that tired of being seen.

Instrument of the Ancestors

TROY L. WIGGINS

Back in the day Darius, Tavis, and Fred would go to Greenbelt Park, stumble down to the banks of the Mississippi, and skip rocks. Even though they weren't supposed to. Darius loved the river, loved the sour smell of ancient rot and the moody, low noises of unseen things splashing in the muddy water. It was their Saturday fall ritual until Fred went under.

"It's like breathing through somebody else's mouth," the Tavis of Darius's memory said from way back. "*Disgusting*, how hot it is outchea."

Fred smiled his goofy, lopsided smile. "Why you thinking about breathing in other boys' mouths? You gay, ain't it, Tavis?"

Fred was right, of course, though Tavis didn't want to admit it. Darius knew that Tavis thought about other boys' mouths all the time. Nobody cared about that. Tavis was Tavis, usually quick with a husky laugh or a soft smile. Except for this time. Instead, his response was to shove Fred. Fred was giggling even when his foot slipped on a piece of crumbling moldy wood, and Darius could still hear crystal clear through the decades the wet slap of Fred's head against a cosmically positioned rock.

They don't remember how the blood trickled down Fred's temple. Just that he fell into the water and was swallowed without a trace. Neither Darius nor Tavis were thinking about other boys' mouths then, at least not in that way. They cussed. They prayed. They ran. What else could they do?

Fred's mother, Harriet, didn't shed a tear at the news.

"The river just takes sometimes," she said. "It gives and it takes, just like the Lord. We got plenty of ancestors in that river. Fred's one of them now. Oh, my baby."

Darius snapped out of his dream and found himself standing in the window of his seventeenth-floor office looking out over the Mississippi River. He didn't even remember approaching the window. He felt half wet, like a towel wrung out and thrown across the floor. His office was full of buzzing, the disquieting clash of cicadas. For a moment he was a boy again, staring in horror at the river that had swallowed his friend.

"*I gets weary and sick of tryin' . . .*"

Something tingled at the edges of his perception, like he wasn't alone. It was his phone, he realized, stumbling to his desk. A 504 area code? You never knew these days. He tapped his earbuds.

"Hello?"

"Hey," a husky voice greeted him. "Is this, uh. Is this Darius Beasley?"

"Yeah, who is . . . wait. *Tavis?*"

"Uh, yeah. I got your number from your mom. How you been?"

"Don't call me after fifteen years with no 'how you been?' What you want?"

Tavis's chuckle incensed Darius even more. "You never did have time for bullshit. But bear with me. Have you, uh. Have you heard from Fred lately?"

"Man, get the fuck off my phone—"

"Wait!" Tavis shouted, and the quaver in his voice made Darius pause. "Man, listen. I know you think I'm bullshitting but I'm serious. You know I been kinda everywhere since I left the city a few years back. I'm in the Gulf working on the oil shit and man, I swear to God I heard Fred's voice calling me. *Body all achin'*, he said. He told me I wouldn't get no rest until Judgment Day."

"Bullshit."

"It wasn't just one day either, man. It was like a month straight. You know his birthday just passed. When the last time you talked to his mom?"

"They put her in that home some years back. But whatever, man. I'm not about to play with you. You ghost for fifteen years and this is what you come back with?"

"I'm serious, D. I'm on a Greyhound heading home. I'll be there in the morning. Will you meet me tomorrow evening? By the river where we used to go? Please? This shit is bugging me, man."

"Whatever," Darius snapped, and ended the call.

Tavis's haunted voice followed Darius home. He was so distracted that he didn't notice the rusty nail on his doorstep until it pierced straight through the sole of his oxfords and into his right foot.

"Goddamnit," he swore, hopping into his house. He threw down his bag and flopped onto his couch, then gently removed his shoe. It'd only barely penetrated the skin—one small bead of blood welled up in the center of his foot. It was rusty, sure, but he didn't want to go to the emergency room tonight. He hit it with some alcohol and wrapped it in gauze. Then he made a little dinner, brushed his teeth, and went to bed.

The voice came to him in the night.

"Show me that stream called the river Jordan
That's the old stream that I long to cross . . ."

Darius normally slept late on Saturdays, but when he woke at 3:45 in the afternoon he saw that Tavis had called six times. He'd sent a couple halting texts as well:

I'm here. At Lamplighter Inn. Goin 2 see ma then headed 2 river.

Meet me there.

Darius turned the request over in his head. Tavis wasn't deserving of forgiveness. But he didn't deserve to be alone. His thoughts were interrupted by someone singing an old song in a boy's voice, an echo of days long gone.

"I get weary and sick of tryin'
I'm tired of livin' an' scared of dyin'"

Darius shot out of bed.

"Fred?" He frantically searched the room. His phone buzzed. It was Tavis.

Headed 2 River.

Meet me there.

"River ain't changed since we was kids," Tavis said, trying to break the silence. It was fall but the bugs and fish were still out. Darius picked up a rock, skimmed it across the thick water. It skipped six, seven times before sinking beneath the surface.

"The fuck you doing here, Tavis? And why you calling me? What you want?"

Tavis shrugged. He looked rough in his oil-spattered coveralls and work boots. His fingernails were black, face gaunt, stubble sickly gray. Darius felt embarrassed in his leather boots and cable-knit sweater.

"You should have stayed," Darius managed. "You should have stayed and dealt with it."

"Like you had to?" Tavis snarled. "I'm not you, and you damn sure ain't me. I couldn't just deal with it. I couldn't stay here."

"Why the fuck not!" Darius advanced on Tavis, shoved him. Tavis was taller than Darius, but leaner. He stumbled over a rock. Both men froze. Brush rustled in the gloomy distance.

"Long low river," a voice echoed off the trees in the low twilight. "It just keeps rolling along."

Both men recognized the voice.

"Fred?" they called.

"No," the voice said. A shrouded figure appeared in the trees. "Fred's gone."

Tavis had produced a knife from his coveralls. Darius motioned for him to put it away. "Stop playing games and show yourself."

The shrouded figure hobbled into view. It wore a long blue raincoat and pulled the hood away to reveal an old woman's face. The two men recognized her instantly.

"Ms. Harriet?" Tavis said. "I don't—"

"Hush your wicked mouth," she said, jabbing a finger at Tavis, who snapped his jaw shut so fast his teeth clicked. Tavis moaned in pain.

"What are you doing out here, Ms. Harriet?" Darius

asked in a whisper. "And how can you speak in Fred's voice?"

"Y'all took him," she murmured, so low that Darius could barely hear her. "Y'all took him and for fifteen years I had to let y'all be until I could find a way to make you pay. But my ancestors showed me how. And it's time."

"Time for what?"

"I didn't need your blood, just for you to step across my hate." At that moment, Darius's right foot throbbed. Ms. Harriet continued. "Fred got no right being my ancestor. But I'll let him use me. I sure will," she said in her own voice. Then, in Fred's:

"*Tote that barge! Lift that bale!*"

Unbidden, the two men's bodies began to move, their bones creaking in protest.

"IknewitIknewit," Tavis whimpered. "Oh Godddddd—"

"They never found my baby. Not one piece of him. But it was never their job to find him."

"Ms. Harriet," Darius said, tears rimming his eyes. "Please—"

"*Not their job*," the old woman shouted, baring her last two teeth that them. "It's yours. *Tote that barge! Lift that bale!*"

"No," Darius gasped as his body shuffled toward the water. It seeped over his ankles, his knees, and it was all he could do to turn to Tavis, who was straining to look at him as well. Tavis's expression was blank, faraway. They were chest-deep when he said:

"I'm tired of living, D. But I'm not scared of dying."

As his head went beneath the surface of the muddy water, Darius heard Ms. Harriet sing in Fred's voice one final time.

"*Pull that rope. Until you dead.*"

Joy, and Other Poisons

VAJRA CHANDRASEKERA

We learn to milk our toxins and history calms the fuck down. Everything's different since the glands were discovered.

Every morning, after we brush our teeth—the gums are too sensitive after the milking—we go out into the world and find a partner. We sit down and we take turns to comb our hair and pick our nits. We unhinge our jaws and put on thick rubber gloves and put our hands in each other's mouth. Some like it barehanded. We stare into our eyes while our hands quest along our gums and press to make each fang come erect.

It has to be done one fang at a time, with plastic

collection vials no larger than a thumb. It takes about half a minute to drain each side, uncomfortable but intimate, and pleasurable in that subdued way left to us after we squeezed fierce joy out of our mouths and poured it down the sink. We are pleasantly anhedonic. It aches a little.

At first we were surprised that the glands and the fangs had gone unnoticed for so many centuries, but then we milked ourselves dry of surprise, too. Everything seems normal now. We take the world in stride.

The primary duct transports toxins to the accessory gland, where forgetfulness is secreted into the mix before it is allowed into the secondary duct, which exits into the hollow solenoglyphous fang. The fang lies flat and hidden when not in use; the human fang is unique in that we use it to bite not only one another but ourselves. We forget bites instantly, losing seconds each time. Our mouths ache for no reason. We think we must have bitten our tongues. The bite may be unconscious or willed: forgetfulness means we can't tell after the fact. It is now believed that historically elevated suicide rates for dentists are due to their being unknowingly bitten too often.

Still, relatively little is known about the nature and mechanism of the glands. The pace of research is slow since we milked ourselves free of burning curiosity and ambition and most of what once constituted individuality, but so is the pace of apocalypse. The discovery of the glands comes too late to save the world, but we are free of grieving. We decide to go gentle into that good night.

We are in no hurry to live or die. We won't have any more children, that's all.

We bow our heads to sea and storm, to the unforgiving sun, the choking air. We have achieved equanimity. We are neither overly excited nor despairing to be the last of our kind.

After each daily milking, we dispose of the collection vials full of clear and dangerous liquid. Most are poured out and the vials recycled. Some are kept for manufacturing antivenom—it's still needed on the front lines, in those few remaining places where deniers hold out against detoxification.

There's a denier enclave near us, too.

Some days we volunteer to fight on the barricades. Some days we picnic by the river. Some days we die, run through by denier bayonets as we try to overwhelm their defenses through sheer numbers. Some days we make love on the riverbank under the beating sun, naked and free. Fear and shame are gone from us.

We have mostly freed ourselves from hope, but we retain enough of it—a little residual pooling in the glands, we think—to believe that the biosphere will thrive once humans are gone. We think it could still be beautiful.

We have no rage, but we have made our decision. The deniers may not be allowed to rebuild the old world, because if let loose again, they will scour the earth to a dry bone.

We still have love, you see—without jealousy or ego. We love the world so much and want it to be well when we're gone. But we know it needs us to be gone.

If the deniers persist in their sorties and their missions and their quests, we will continue to swarm their barricades in our millions.

If the deniers keep sending us courage-crazed heroes, we will hold them down with a hundred hands and milk them free. So many of us started out that way. We remember the moments our hearts cleared and we looked up at the sea of calm faces above us, the gentle hands deep in our unhinged mouths.

We will never stop coming. We know they think of us as the monsters.

Visiting Hours

LILLIAM RIVERA

R ight before the nurse wheels her man in to surgery, Vilma's stomach growls loudly. She rests her hand on her extended belly as if she can comfort the growing baby inside. The gesture does nothing. Instead, her stomach barks back. Nothing can ever quell this hunger no matter how hard she tries to stay atop it.

"Shut up," Vilma mutters under her breath.

The anesthetician gives her a condescending look, the look she's been receiving ever since she arrived at the hospital at the crack of dawn to check him in.

"We'll take good care of him," the anesthetician says, although Vilma hadn't asked a question. Isn't it their job to take care of him?

Vilma's boyfriend, Rogelio, stares at the ceiling. He doesn't look at Vilma, as if by doing so the hard exterior he's spent years cultivating will break down. The man who has it all under control. The one who whispered, "I'll take care of you," when he found out Vilma was pregnant. Even back then she thought of leaving his ass and still wishes she had but now it's too late. She's stuck with Rogelio, his clogged-up arteries, and this hungry beast inside her for who knows how long.

"We have your phone number. We'll call you when we're done," the nurse says. She hands Vilma saltine crackers and motions for her to go. "Don't forget to drink water."

The baby in her belly kicks as if the nurse is talking to him. Vilma doesn't say bye to Rogelio. He wouldn't respond to her even if she did. He's too busy trying not to freak out. She should at least offer him a prayer. Something. Instead she walks to the waiting room.

The room is filled with people. Families jostle to find an outlet to charge their phones. The television is tuned to the morning show, where everyone is way too chatty and happy.

"Here, please sit down." A man offers his seat. She declines. She doesn't want to sit even though her ankles are swollen. Vilma doesn't want any part of it. They said it would take two hours for the surgery. *Roughly*, they said. Two hours in this hospital with these people. She can feel it. Their anxiety.

Vilma tears open the crackers and eats. The baby calms down. She finds a seat a short distance from the waiting room in a quieter section. The only people walking through this area are the nurses' aids taking their break and whispering into their phones. A black-and-white picture of Judy Garland hangs on the wall facing Vilma. The actress wears heavy eyeliner and a cigarette dangles lazily from her hand. She leans against Mickey Rooney, her face worn and tired. Vilma wonders who decided this picture of a trash-looking Dorothy would be the feel-good decoration for a hospital. Vilma can see her own reflection in the framed picture. She's still angry at her short cut, a display of rage after Rogelio told her about the surgery. The baby kicks again. She tries to nudge the ravenous thing away from what feels like her ribs. She can barely breathe. How much longer does she have to endure it before this creature leaves her?

An old woman sits right next to Vilma although there are plenty of empty seats around her. The woman wears worn bedroom slippers from which her toes poke out. Her toenails are long and stained black. The oversized denim jacket that covers her multiple shirts is much too big for her small frame. The woman clasps tightly to the chair as if she's on a ride.

"You shouldn't be here," the woman says. "This is a bad place for a baby."

The woman's voice sounds familiar in a way that Vilma can't quite place. Her breath smells of eggs. The stench is so strong and Vilma can feel her nausea rising.

"I don't care. I don't care about this baby or this stupid hospital," Vilma says, annoyed. "He said he would take care of us. I should have known. Trapped with this freaking thing inside me."

Vilma's ankles throb from standing too long. She should move but she won't. The old woman's breathing is as labored as Vilma's. They both sit staring at the picture of Judy Garland for a long time.

Rogelio's surgeon wears black sneakers. When he walks toward her and the old lady, the sneakers make a squeaking sound.

"There was so much scar tissue, my instrument bent," the surgeon says. Vilma tries to picture that, a knife bending inside Rogelio's chest.

"Your husband aged me twenty years," the surgeon says with a chuckle. Vilma doesn't laugh. "You can both see him in recovery soon."

"She's not with me," Vilma says. The doctor doesn't hear her. He continues telling her details from the surgery she doesn't understand. When the doctor leaves, the old lady mutters to herself. Vilma gets up and the old lady stays looking at the photo.

The sight of his tears sickens her. He was supposed to be tending to her, not the other way around.

"Please don't leave me," Rogelio says. He won't stop.

"We can get a cot for you," the nurse offers, and now it's official. Vilma will spend the night in the hospital.

Vilma swore she would never get sucked into the sameness. Rogelio was fun at first. They did the wildest things.

Then he kept eating everything. She couldn't stand to hear him chew with his mouth open.

The cot is uncomfortable and her stomach won't stop making noises. Rogelio is out cold, high on drugs she can't even pronounce. Vilma stands and walks to the vending machine. The empty waiting room feels off. She inserts a couple of dollar bills and selects a Snickers bar.

Who made this decision to live this life? she thinks. How did she fall down this hole? Vilma walks up to the Judy Garland photo, and with her finger smears a little bit of chocolate on Judy's face. There's a sound of shuffling behind her.

"Don't you have a home?" Vilma snaps. She doesn't like being spied on. Doesn't want to continue to smell the sourness of this stranger's body. She doesn't want any of this—the hospital, that stupid cot, this greedy parasite inside her, and this moment right now.

"I know what to do," the old woman says.

She reaches out and touches Vilma's belly.

"A hospital isn't a place for a baby," she says.

Vilma's stomach no longer growls with hunger. Instead, there's a stillness so unsettling that Vilma gasps.

The old woman just smiles.

Parakeets

KEVIN BROCKMEIER

Not long ago there lived a man with three pet parakeets: the first appareled in jewel tones of green and yellow, the second with a blue brow that faded into a creamy purple breast, and the third an albino with a beanbag-like belly. Every day from dawn to dusk their chattering permeated the man's sunroom, all blond wood and arched windows. It was the most calming space in the house, his sunroom, but for a single perplexing defect—a frigid patch against the back wall, roughly the size of a water tank. How was it, the man wondered, that even in high summer, at three thirty in the afternoon, when his shirt was pasted to his back with sweat, he would feel an alarming chill whenever he passed behind the sofa and to the immediate left of his credenza? Sometimes, walking in or out of the room, he would pause before he had emerged from the temperature

KEVIN BROCKMEIER

well just to appreciate the sense of disorientation it caused him: two-thirds of his body warm and comfortable, yet the ice lopping off an arm or a leg, a slice of his foot, the escarpment of his shoulder. One day the man was polishing his hardwoods when, to access a section of the floor, he moved the birdcage into the cold patch. A silence enshrouded the birds. Their feathers flattened. Whether through tiredness or simple absentmindedness, the man neglected to restore the cage to its spot in the corner, and by the next morning, when he returned, the perches and wires were covered in a verdigris of frost. As he approached, the parakeets stood at attention. Try as he might, he had never been able to extend their vocabulary beyond a few basic words: *birdseed*, *not-now*, *pretty-bird*, *night-night*. Yet now, so quietly he would not have heard them if the air conditioner had not clicked off, the first bird said, "I do not know where I am." And the second said, "I deserve another chance." And "The wind here is so bitter and it never stops," said the albino. The man felt as if someone had emptied a breath onto the nape of his neck. A marshy smell rose from his armpits. He had always enjoyed riddles, even insoluble ones, but there were riddles and then there were riddles. He instructed himself to move the cage back to the corner. *Do it. Do it.* But the cold of the copper bit his fingers to the skeleton. He flinched. He backed away. Without thinking, because he had said it so many times before, he asked, "Who's a pretty bird?" The parakeets eyed him with a daunting directness. "Is someone there? Will you speak up? Let us out. Come closer. I can

almost hear you. Come closer. Come closer. Let us out."
Between the bars of the cage everything was green and yellow like the grass at daybreak, or blue and violet like the last
brush of the evening, or fat and white like the sun pinned
in the sky, until he reached for the latch and the darkness
rushed in.

Permissions Acknowledgments

About the Editors

LINCOLN MICHEL is the author of *Upright Beasts*, a collection of genre-bending stories from Coffee House Press. His work appears in *The Paris Review*, *The New York Times*, *Strange Horizons*, *Granta*, *The Guardian*, the Pushcart Prize anthology, and elsewhere. With Nadxieli Nieto, he is the editor of *Tiny Crimes* and *Gigantic Worlds*. He teaches fiction writing at Columbia University and Sarah Lawrence College. You can find him online at lincolnmichel.com.

NADXIELI NIETO is the editor of *Tiny Crimes* and *Gigantic Worlds* with Lincoln Michel, and *Carteles Contra Una Guerra*. She was formerly the managing editor of *NOON* annual and editor in chief of *Salt Hill*. Her work has appeared in *BuzzFeed*, *Vice*, *New York Tyrant*, and elsewhere. Her collaborative artist books may be found in the collections of the Museum of Modern Art and the Brooklyn Museum.

About the Contributors

SELENA GAMBRELL ANDERSON's work has appeared or is forthcoming in *Oxford American, The Georgia Review, Bomb, Callaloo, Fence*, and *Best American Short Stories 2020*. She has received fellowships from the Kimbilio Center, the MacDowell Colony, and the Bread Loaf Writers' Conference, and recently won a Rona Jaffe Foundation Writers' Award. She lives in San Francisco with her family and is working on a novel.

J. S. BREUKELAAR is the author of the collection *Collision: Stories* and the novels *Aletheia* and *American Monster*. Her new novel, *The Bridge*, will be released in early 2021. You can find her fiction and nonfiction at *Gamut, Lightspeed, Black Static, Juked, Volume 1 Brooklyn*, and elsewhere. She teaches writing at LitReactor.com and at the University of Sydney, in Australia, where she lives with her family.

KEVIN BROCKMEIER is the author of eight volumes of fiction and one memoir. His most recent book, from which "Parakeets" is taken, is *The Ghost Variations: One Hundred Stories*. He teaches frequently at the Iowa Writers' Workshop and lives in Little Rock, Arkansas, where he was raised.

ABOUT THE CONTRIBUTORS

CHASE BURKE is the author of the fiction chapbook *Lecture*, published as a winner of the Paper Nautilus Debut Series. Elsewhere, his stories appear in *Glimmer Train*, *Salt Hill*, and *Sycamore Review*, among other journals. Burke has an MFA from the University of Alabama, where he was the fiction editor of *Black Warrior Review*. He lives in Florida and is working on a collection of stories and a novel. You can find him at chaseburke.com.

AMRITA CHAKRABORTY is a Bangladeshi American writer. Her work has been published by *Kajal Magazine*, *BOAAT*, *Split Lip Magazine*, and *The Tempest*, among other publications. She is on the staff of *Half Mystic* journal, and was a winner of the 2018 Golden Shovel Poetry Prize. She is working on her first novel.

VAJRA CHANDRASEKERA is from Colombo, Sri Lanka. His work has appeared in *Analog*, *Clarkesworld*, and *Nightmare*, among other publications. You can find him online at vajra.me.

WHITNEY COLLINS's debut story collection, *Big Bad*, received the 2019 Mary McCarthy Prize in Short Fiction and is forthcoming from Sarabande Books in 2021. Collins is a 2020 Pushcart Prize winner ("The Entertainer") and a 2020 Pushcart Prize Special Mention ("The Pupil"). Her fiction has appeared in *New Ohio Review*, *Grist*, *The Pinch*, *The*

Chattahoochee Review, Ninth Letter, and *Southeast Review,* among other publications. She lives in Kentucky.

JOSH COOK is the author of the novel *An Exaggerated Murder,* published by Melville House in March 2015. His fiction and other work has appeared in the *Coe Review, Epicenter, Owen Wister Review, Barge, Plume Anthology of Poetry* 2012 and 2013, and elsewhere. He was a finalist in the 2011 and 2012 Cupboard Pamphlet fiction contest. He is a bookseller with Porter Square Books in Cambridge, Massachusetts.

MEG ELISON is a science fiction author and feminist essayist. Her series, *The Road to Nowhere,* won the 2014 Philip K. Dick Award. She was a James Tiptree, Jr. Literary Award honoree in 2018. In 2020, she published her first collection, *Big Girl,* with PM Press and her first young adult novel, *Find Layla,* with Skyscape. Elison has been published in *McSweeney's, Fantasy & Science Fiction, Fangoria,* and many other places. She is a high school dropout and a graduate of UC Berkeley.

BRIAN EVENSON has published over a dozen books of fiction, most recently *Song for the Unraveling of the World.* His novel *Last Days* was a 2010 ALA/RUSA-recommended book, and his novel *The Open Curtain* was a finalist for an Edgar Award. His story collection *The Wavering Knife* won the International Horror Guild Award. A new collection,

The Glassy Burning Floor of Hell, which includes this story, will appear in 2021. He is a 2017 Guggenheim Fellow. He lives in Los Angeles and teaches at CalArts.

COREY FARRENKOPF lives on Cape Cod with his wife, Gabrielle, and works as a librarian. His fiction has been published in *Redivider*, *Catapult*, *Hobart*, *Monkeybicycle*, *Volume 1 Brooklyn*, *Slush Pile Magazine*, *Third Point Press*, *Cotton Xenomorph*, and elsewhere. To learn more, follow him on twitter @CoreyFarrenkopf or on the web at CoreyFarrenkopf.com

IVÁN PARRA GARCIA holds an MFA in Spanish Creative Writing from the University of Iowa, where he was the editor in chief of *Iowa Literaria*. His stories and essays have been published in Spanish and English in *Litro*, *Revista Leer*, *Suburbano*, *Al filo del Pensamiento*, and *Shahrazad Press*. He is the author of *Texarkana*, a collection of short stories, and lives in Ann Arbor, Michigan. You can find him at iparragarcia.com.

RACHEL HENG is the author of the novel *Suicide Club*, which won the Gladstone Library Writers in Residence Award 2020 and will be translated into ten languages worldwide. Heng's short fiction has received a Pushcart Prize Special Mention and *Prairie Schooner*'s Jane Geske Award and has appeared in *Glimmer Train*, *Guernica*, *McSweeney's Quarterly*, *Kenyon Review*, and elsewhere.

THERESA HOTTEL was born in Taipei and raised in southern Oklahoma, and writes about ghosts, women, and landscape. Her fiction appears in *No Tokens Journal*, *SmokeLong Quarterly*, and *Volume 1 Brooklyn*, and she has received support from Art Omi: Writers, Bread Loaf Environmental Writers' Conference, and Homestead National Monument, among other organizations. She holds an MFA from Columbia University and is at work on her first novel.

SAMANTHA HUNT is the author of the short story collection *The Dark Dark* and three novels: *Mr. Splitfoot*, a ghost story; *The Invention of Everything Else*, about the life of inventor Nikola Tesla; and *The Seas*. She is the recipient of a Guggenheim Fellowship, the Bard Fiction Prize, the National Book Foundation's 5 Under 35 Prize, the St. Francis College Literary Prize, and a finalist for the Orange Prize and the PEN/Faulkner. Hunt teaches at Pratt Institute.

PEDRO INIGUEZ lives in Eagle Rock, California, a quiet community in Northeast Los Angeles. Since childhood he has been fascinated with science fiction, horror, and comic books. His work can be found in various magazines and anthologies, including *Space and Time Magazine*, *Crossed Genres*, *Dig Two Graves*, *Writers of Mystery and Imagination*, *Deserts of Fire*, and *Altered States II*. His cyberpunk novel, *Control Theory*, was released in 2016. He can be found online at pedroiniguezauthor.com.

ABOUT THE CONTRIBUTORS

JAC JEMC teaches creative writing at the University of California San Diego. She is the author of five books of fiction, including *The Grip of It* and *False Bingo*.

STEPHEN GRAHAM JONES is the author of sixteen and a half novels, six story collections, a couple of novellas, and a couple of one-shot comic books. Most recent works are *Mapping the Interior* and *My Hero*. Next are *The Only Good Indians* and *Night of the Mannequins*. Jones lives and teaches in Boulder, Colorado.

DAEHYUN KIM has exhibited widely in solo and group exhibitions in South Korea, Hong Kong, New York, Miami, Paris, London, Bangkok, Singapore, Oslo, and Romania. He was trained in the traditional painting techniques of Korean Art and studied East Asian art history, graduating with a BFA in Oriental Painting from Hongik University.

LINDSAY KING-MILLER is the author of *Ask a Queer Chick: A Guide to Sex, Love, and Life for Girls Who Dig Girls*. She lives in Denver with her partner and two children.

MONIQUE LABAN is a fiction writer and essayist based in New York. Her nonfiction has appeared in *Electric Literature* and *Catapult*. She is an alumna of the 2019 Tin House Summer Workshop, the 2019 Viable Paradise

Workshop, and the 2017 Voices of Our Nation Arts (VONA) Workshop.

HILARY LEICHTER is the author of the novel *Temporary*. Her writing has appeared in *n+1*, *Harper's Magazine*, *The New Yorker*, *Bookforum*, and *Conjunctions*. She lives in Brooklyn, New York.

BEN LOORY is the author of the collections *Tales of Falling and Flying* and *Stories for Nighttime and Some for the Day*. His fables and tales have appeared in *The New Yorker*, *Tin House*, *The Sewanee Review*, and *A Public Space*, and on *This American Life* and *Selected Shorts*.

CANISIA LUBRIN is a St. Lucian Canadian writer, editor, critic, and teacher published and anthologized internationally, with translations of her work in Spanish, Italian, French, and German. Her poetry debut, *Voodoo Hypothesis*, was named a CBC Best Book and garnered multiple award nominations. *The Dyzgraphxst* is her second poetry book. "Cedar Grove Rose" is part of *Code Noir*, her in-progress short story collection. Lubrin holds an MFA from the University of Guelph.

JEI D. MARCADE is a Korean American speculative fiction writer whose work has appeared in *sub-Q*, *Uncanny Magazine*, and *Strange Horizons*, among other publications.

They can be found haunting jeidmarcade.com or tweeting sporadically at @JeiDMarcade.

HELEN MCCLORY is the author of *On the Edges of Vision*, *Mayhem & Death*, and *The Goldblum Variations*. There is a moor and a cold sea in her heart.

SAM J. MILLER is the last in a long line of butchers. He is the Nebula Award–winning author of *The Art of Starving* (an NPR best of the year) and *Blackfish City* (Nebula finalist and winner of the hopefully-soon-to-be-renamed John W. Campbell Memorial Award). A graduate of the Clarion Science Fiction & Fantasy Writers' Workshop, Miller lives in New York City.

ALANA MOHAMED is a writer and librarian from Queens, New York. She is currently working on a short story collection, as well as a collection of essays about running late to the proverbial party.

RICHIE NARVAEZ is the author of two novels, *Hipster Death Rattle* and *Holly Hernandez and the Death of Disco*, as well as two collections of short fiction, *Roachkiller and Other Stories*, which won the Spinetingler Award for Best Anthology/ Short Story Collection, and *Noiryorican*. He teaches at the Fashion Institute of Technology in Manhattan and lives in the Bronx.

KEVIN NGUYEN is the author of *New Waves*. He lives in Brooklyn, New York.

ALLANA C. NOYES is a literary translator from Reno, Nevada. She holds an MFA from the University of Iowa and was a Fulbright fellow in Mexico. In 2018, she was the winner of the World Literature Today Translation Prize in Poetry, and, in 2020, was selected for the emerging translator fellowship at the Banff Centre. Her translations have appeared in *Asymptote*, *Lunch Ticket*, *Exchanges*, *Litro*, and elsewhere.

SHELLY ORIA is the author of *New York 1, Tel Aviv 0*; the co-author, with Alice Sola Kim, of the digital novella *CLEAN*; and the editor of *Indelible in the Hippocampus: Writings from the Me Too Movement*. Her fiction has appeared in *The Paris Review* and elsewhere, has been translated into other languages, and has won a number of awards. Oria lives in Brooklyn, New York, where she has a private practice as a life and creativity coach.

LILLIAM RIVERA is the author of the young adult novels *Dealing in Dreams*, *The Education of Margot Sanchez*, and *Never Look Back*. Her work has appeared in *The New York Times*, *The Washington Post*, and *Elle*, among other publications. Rivera lives in Los Ángeles.

JOSEPH SALVATORE is the author of *To Assume a Pleasing Shape* and the coauthor of *Understanding English Grammar*.

He is the books editor at *The Brooklyn Rail* and has published work in *The New York Times Book Review*, *Los Angeles Times*, *The Collagist*, *Dossier*, *Epiphany*, *New York Tyrant*, *Open City*, *Post Road*, *Salt Hill*, *Rain Taxi*, *Routledge International Encyclopedia of Queer Culture*, and *The Believer Logger*. An associate professor at The New School, he founded their journal, *LIT*.

RION AMILCAR SCOTT is the author of the story collection *The World Doesn't Require You*. His debut story collection, *Insurrections*, was awarded the 2017 PEN/Bingham Prize for Debut Fiction and the 2017 Hillsdale Award from the Fellowship of Southern Writers. His work has been published in journals such as *The New Yorker*, *Kenyon Review*, *Crab Orchard Review*, and *The Rumpus*, among other publications.

BENNETT SIMS is the author of the novel *A Questionable Shape* and the collection *White Dialogues*. His fiction has appeared in *A Public Space*, *Conjunctions*, and Electric Literature, and his work has received the Bard Fiction Prize, a Pushcart Prize, and the Joseph Brodsky Rome Prize from the American Academy in Rome. He teaches fiction at the University of Iowa.

AMBER SPARKS is the author of *The Unfinished World: And Other Stories* and *And I Do Not Forgive You: Stories and Other*

Revenges, both from Liveright. Her fiction and essays have appeared in *Tin House, Granta, The Cut, The Paris Review,* and other publications.

ANDREW F. SULLIVAN is the author of the novel *Waste* and the short story collection *All We Want Is Everything.* His fiction has appeared in *Hazlitt, The New Quarterly, Beneath Ceaseless Skies,* and other publications. Sullivan lives in Hamilton, Ontario, where he works at an urban planning and design firm.

ESHANI SURYA is a writer based in Greenville, South Carolina. Her writing has appeared in or is forthcoming in *Catapult, Paper Darts, Joyland,* and *Literary Hub,* among other publications. She was the 2016 winner of the Ryan R. Gibbs Award for Flash Fiction from *New Delta Review.* Surya is also a Flash Fiction Reader at *Split Lip Magazine.* She holds an MFA from the University of Arizona in Tucson. Find her online at @__eshani.

LENA VALENCIA's fiction has appeared in *CRAFT, Joyland, The Masters Review, 7x7 LA,* and elsewhere. She teaches at Catapult, the Sackett Street Writers' Workshop, and *One Story,* where she is also the managing editor. She is the recipient of a 2019 Elizabeth George Foundation Grant and received her MFA in fiction from The New School.

ABOUT THE CONTRIBUTORS

MATTHEW VOLLMER is the author of *Future Missionaries of America*, *Inscriptions for Headstones*, *Gateway to Paradise*, and *Permanent Exhibit*. He teaches at Virginia Tech.

TROY L. WIGGINS is an award-winning writer and editor from Memphis, Tennessee. His short fiction and essays have appeared in *Long Hidden: Speculative Fiction from the Margins of History*, *Memphis Noir*, *Fireside Magazine*, *Memphis Flyer*, PEN America, and on Tor.com. Wiggins formerly edited the World Fantasy Award–winning *FIYAH Magazine of Black Speculative Fiction*, and is the 2019 Coger Memorial Hall of Fame inductee for his contributions to speculative fiction in Memphis.

CHAVISA WOODS is the author of four books, including the short fiction collection *Things to Do When You're Goth in the Country* and *100 Times: A Memoir of Sexism*. Woods is a MacDowell Fellow and was the recipient of the Shirley Jackson Award in 2018, the Acker Award in writing, the Cobalt Prize for fiction, and was a three-time Lambda Literary Award finalist for fiction. Her work has received praise from *The New York Times*, *Publishers Weekly*, *The Stranger*, *The Seattle Review of Books*, *Booklist*, *Electric Literature*, *PopMatters*, *The Rumpus*, *The Library Journal*, and many other publications.

MICHELE ZIMMERMAN is a queer writer with an MFA in fiction from Sarah Lawrence College. Her work appears in *Lockjaw Magazine, Psychopomp,* and other publications. Two of her short stories have been Top-25 Finalists for the *Glimmer Train* Short Story Award for New Writers, and in 2018 she was a Sundress Publications Best of the Net nominee. She lives with her partner and their two cats.

Index